Praise for Joanne McNeil

"A strange, surprising, and sinister kaleidoscope of a novel. Joanne McNeil, with dazzling wit and an eye for detail, guides us through a capitalist gig-economy world both relatable and startlingly visionary. *Wrong Way* stands out sparklingly from the crowd of current novels. I found myself describing it, recommending it, to a person on the subway I barely knew. I really love this book."

—Scott Heim, author of *Mysterious Skin*

"With her signature mix of intelligent, tender, and engaging prose, Joanne McNeil has written a brilliant novel in *Wrong Way*, which interrogates the promises of the tech utopia through the lives of the invisible labor behind the hype."

—Zito Madu, author of
The Minotaur at Calla Lanza

Lizzy Johnston

Joanne McNeil
Wrong Way

Joanne McNeil is the author of *Lurking: How a Person Became a User*. She was the inaugural winner of the Carl & Marilynn Thoma Foundation's Arts Writing Award for emerging writers. She has been a resident at Eyebeam, a Logan Nonfiction Program fellow, and an instructor at the School for Poetic Computation. She grew up in Brockton, Massachusetts.

Also by Joanne McNeil

Lurking: How a Person Became a User

Wrong Way

Wrong Way

Joanne McNeil

Wrong Way

MCD × FSG Originals

Farrar, Straus and Giroux   New York

MCD × FSG Originals
Farrar, Straus and Giroux
120 Broadway, New York 10271

Library of Congress Cataloging-in-Publication Data
Names: McNeil, Joanne, author.
Title: Wrong way / Joanne McNeil.
Description: First edition. | New York : MCD x FSG Originals /
    Farrar, Straus and Giroux, 2023.
Identifiers: LCCN 2023021276 | ISBN 9780374610661 (paperback)
Subjects: LCGFT: Novels.
Classification: LCC PS3613.C58598 W76 2023 | DDC 813/.6—
    dc23/eng/20230707
LC record available at https://lccn.loc.gov/2023021276

Designed by Abby Kagan

Our books may be purchased in bulk for promotional, educational, or
business use. Please contact your local bookseller or the Macmillan
Corporate and Premium Sales Department at 1-800-221-7945, extension
5442, or by email at MacmillanSpecialMarkets@macmillan.com.

www.fsgoriginals.com • www.mcdbooks.com
Follow us on Twitter, Facebook, and Instagram at @fsgoriginals

10 9 8 7 6 5 4 3 2 1

Wrong Way

Some of them were good jobs. All of them were odd. Each was better than nothing, but it's true, some were not bad and a few jobs were even good. A steady paycheck and a sense of purpose made all the difference.

There were those evenings and weekends behind the jewelry counter at Cedars department store. It was good. She could walk there. That's what everyone wants, right? To walk to work. She didn't know it then. The walk was unscenic alongside traffic that choked at splintering intersections through a district of thin streets laid down sometime late in the seventeenth century. First a cow hoofed it, disrupted a field and kicked up dandelions and weeds. Then a path was set, and, in turn, it became a dirt cartway before it was paved with granite sett. Bluestone sidewalks came later, and even later, a blacktop layer. The old stones underneath, buried for decades, now reveal themselves to the modern world at the street corners where the asphalt is cracked.

Downtown had the density of a city neighborhood and none of the sprawl of the suburb it was, but it was no city. Each shop had the same olive lighting, the same eggs-and-sawdust smell and old circulars from *The Patriot Ledger*, stepped on and crusted over where the threshold ramps met the sidewalk. There was a family-owned hardware store, a package store, and a store that sold crystal figures and stationery—Christian stuff, Bible verses carved in pewter, and wind chimes and dream catchers, possibly, but it was hard to tell from the window display. Once she went inside the army navy store because a magazine said that's where you could get nice peacoats for cheap. They had no peacoats. Or maybe they did, she didn't want to ask or stick around long. There were three people inside hanging around the cash register and they all looked like old vets.

She would cross at the Cumberland Farms next to Stoughton's lone Chinese restaurant. Cedars glowed like a fallen star that crashed into the parking lot, a beacon of warm light in the evening fog beaming through the frosted-glass brick that wrapped around the exterior. Grid patterns and shapes were painted on the walls in primary colors like trigonometry homework completed with a four-color Bic. The orderly displays inside summoned a clientele just as structured. It was a catalog showroom. Customers knew what they wanted before they got there. Sometimes they went to the store to see an object in person that they had circled in the glossy wish book that arrived at their front doors with a thud like the Yellow Pages. There would be a specific model of vacuum cleaner or a top-of-the-line car phone in a zip-up bag that they were curious about. They'd find the right department, decide to make a purchase or not, and then return to their cars somewhere in the pothole-speckled lot. Nurses bought Keds sneakers, sometimes three pairs of the same style at a time. Guys from the auto body shop across the road might stop in for replacement pliers. No one experienced the store from one end to the other except for the children who scurried off when their moms asked one of the sales associates about a digital alarm clock warranty or their dads checked the prices of the coffee makers in stock. But even those kids tended to flock to the same place—the lighting department. They'd find the best spot: looking up from underneath the display of chandeliers with stained glass torch lamps in staggered heights and ceramic table lamps crowding the shelves on either side.

There was an office in the center of the building, a place the staff called the "heart" of the store. In these secret rooms, the floors were solid white tile and dusty. The walls were plain. She'd tap in at the punch clock and stuff a paper bag with her name on it with the other paper bags in the mini fridge in the kitchen where the lights constantly flickered off and on.

Her heels would tap gently on the tiles as she followed the central artery toward her station. Thin red dotted lines and thick blue squares accenting the checkerboard floors like trail markers. The fluorescent lights blanched the counter vitrines from a distance. She felt like an actor in a stage play; a leading role in a team effort and public-facing too. Curtain up was when she typed in her code for the cash register: 7485. Her department was in between hardware and cosmetics. At the start of her shift, she could smell the metallic of brand-new wrenches and synthetic tuberose house perfume on either side; it felt right for the glittering baubles pinned to groves on beige velvet slabs, beautiful small things locked in glass like tropical fish in an aquarium.

She carried the vitrines key on a neon spiral lanyard around her wrist. It made her feel important.

The job was dull most of the time. Dull is not bad. If it had been an actual theater performance, she would have had to stand around and wait through rehearsals and breaks too. She felt safe behind the counter. No one could get too close to her.

The best customers were the people who bought pendants. That's a neutral gift. Middle-aged women would buy silver stars on silver chains for their best friends. There were pin-size ladybug pendants that grandmothers liked to get for their grandchildren. No one ever bought the Hasbro charm necklace with dangling Monopoly pieces, but some of the kids, who wandered to the counter on their own from the VCR section or the lawn mower display, would come by and ask for it.

"Lemme!!" shouted an unaccompanied four-year-old, her eyes focused on the brassy chain with a slight tangle between the wheelbarrow charm and Scottie dog. Teresa didn't mind it. She asked the little girl to turn around, secured the clasp, and let her hold the old-fashioned hand mirror that they kept behind the counter, so the child could admire the shiny pieces around her neck.

Bracelets were boring. It was exhausted-looking men in suits who would arrive at the store at quarter to six and ask to see the "tennis bracelets." They would quickly decide on one of several identical thin chains with some ambivalence and run out once they paid. Rings were something else: statement pieces, tended for sentimental reasons. She sold about three claddagh rings a week. All the customers were buying for someone else, so they often asked for her opinion of the inventory. She didn't like Cedars jewelry—or any jewelry, or anything unnecessary—but she studied it all in the pamphlets tucked under the register that explained cuts and clarity. She learned every birthstone and remembered the advice from her coworkers, things like how customers liked to pretend that sapphire was the gemstone for December. Just let them.

"You're not going to find anything nicer than that," she'd say. That was one of her lines. She sold six engagement rings and only two of the six men tried to flirt with her. Each ring was about a forty-dollar commission.

She thought, when the first commission on an engagement ring sale hit her paycheck, that she was lucky. By the sixth ring, she figured she was going to be the kind of person who would never struggle with money. It would just happen and come easily. Already she was making it.

She wore no rings, no earrings, nothing herself. The customers never seemed to notice. But when she first started, she tried on jewelry when no one was looking. She'd slide an engagement ring onto her left ring finger and then onto her right. It wasn't in the pamphlets, which hand the ring was for; on either hand, the diamonds always looked wrong on the girl's finger. In the gemstone vitrine, there was a horizontal egg-shaped garnet ring that looked antique. She liked it enough and thought it would be a nice keepsake kind of thing to have to remember this moment in time. It was fifty-six dollars, a lot, but her plan was to buy it after her tenth engagement ring commission and she'd still have all that money left over. The store discount was 20 percent off; maybe, she thought, she'd even get to keep the commission if she rang it up herself.

On her fifteen-minute break, she strolled through the aisles with color swatches for house paint. She daydreamed about living on her own and painting the ceiling a specific shade of cloudy powder blue: Windmill Wings. She had another spiral wristlet with a key for the closet-size room behind the juniors section. There, she'd switch out VHS tapes that played on nine televisions mounted above racks of jeans and cropped T-shirts. Each tape played music videos for two hours. On one VHS player, she'd enter a new tape, and on the other, she'd set the completed tape to rewind. Sometimes the key-cutting machine in hardware would screech over the music. Elsewhere there were speakers constantly playing wordless music that was diaphanous and jazzy. She only noticed it when the televisions stopped and it was time to switch out the VHS tapes.

Her boss seemed so old. He was only twenty-five, but he was married, but he also didn't act like it. There were a few times she didn't like the way he looked at her, but even contemplating this many years later, in the pool, lap sixteen, she thought that look she didn't like was that of a disgruntled vaunter who would have preferred to be, as he probably is today, selling snowmobiles or pontoons or something bigger, with the risks and rewards to show for it. Absent any real power, he focused on irrelevant tasks, staging his subordinate like a mannequin and reminding her to smile. This was the first thing a customer would have seen from the center left entrance: a teenage girl with her dark hair to her waist and a muted smile, dressed in her nicest clothes—plaid skirts, black tights, cardigan sets—clean ensembles made of synthetic fabrics, first-day-back-at-school attire, the clothes she could wear to church; quiet behind a glass counter, under panels of powerful incandescent daylight-mimicking lights.

She loved the thirty minutes between closing and lockup. Counting the cash, then placing it in a leather pouch with the most expensive inventory in the safe. Loved that the store trusted her to do this. When the central lights went out, the whole place felt serene; it was still brighter than anything in town, still a crashed star in the lot. She never did get that garnet ring. She was sixteen years old.

Lap sixteen at the Y is when she would remember this, flip turn, and recall, before seventeen, how the job ended. It was a good job, but those stores don't exist now. Those jobs don't.

Lap seventeen. She was no mannequin there, dressed in a wrinkly and oversized polo with the convenience store logo above the right breast. Hunched over and amorphous, like all the customers, but she was twenty years younger than the youngest among them. She can't remember much of it. Still. Not a bad job. She could walk there.

A good job at eighteen. Lap eighteen. The workplace was good. She got to eat for free in the cafeteria with all the technical workers. Most of them had thick black-frame glasses and severe haircuts. It was some dot-com, some sort of creative agency. It surprised her to see cool-looking people in this suburb—Norwood; she thought people like that all lived in Boston. She was whisked to a tiny room with no windows to read a script in a cubicle in the dark; what it was, she can't remember now, just selling people over the phone on whatever the company was selling. That was not good. But it was good on her lunch breaks. Fresh pastas and salads. Really good food. They asked her for a four-digit PIN to log in to see the call registry. She already remembered 7485. On a ten-key, it was as easy to type as anything at all.

Lap nineteen and careful not to blink so her goggles don't leak. Data entry at the Paper Mason headquarters in a crumbling neo-Romanesque tower in Brockton with an ornate arched roof and graffiti on the sides. It smelled funny in there, like the kitchen fridge needed a deep clean. Another time, they asked for a four-digit pin: 7485. Lap twenty, lap twenty-one, lap twenty-two. Something at the Milton country club. It was only for the summer. Pouring wine, sweeping up. It was fine, the money was good: minimum wage on paper, a W-2, but she cleaned up in tips. Other jobs. Lap twenty-five is when things changed. That's when the money really made a difference. She lets her mind wander until it's two miles almost, lap fifty-one and out. She can swim longer than her years. Up in the cold air, nothing to hear but splashing and echoes. Toweling off. She removes her cap and squeezes her wet chin-length hair. There were other jobs that were not so good.

2

Teresa has her head pressed against the window of the white shuttle bus. Her forehead vibrates and her teeth chatter with the rumble. The bus hums into her knees and her feet absorb the trembling floor. The seats feel damp while the AC is cranked to the max against the sound of the engine; all is silent besides. A few of the seat cushions are held together with duct tape. It's morning, early August and already hot at this hour with a faint wind gust that will greet the arrivals when they step off one by one. Just a touch of relief.

Out the window, she can see the same cracked asphalt where she once walked to work in cheap heels. But the summer morning light casts a disorienting haze over the town. It is always fall or winter in Stoughton when Teresa remembers it. Could that be where the strange Bible store once was? She slides closer to the side of the bus as the driver turns the other way.

This could be a good job. At South Station thirty minutes earlier, the fifty passengers in this vehicle had been waiting in an ambiguous crowd, each of them unsure whether they were in the right place; mixed in with strangers who would stay strange—the travelers gripping duffel bags and suitcases on caster wheels, who had stopped to review directions to the hotel, Logan Airport, or wherever happened to be the next leg of their journeys. The expectant workers grazed a few feet from one another as a loose crowd of a couple dozen people grew to a concentrated shape. They were middle-aged, mostly, but some older and some much younger. A diverse crowd, otherwise. Teresa noticed in their faces some expression of anxiety in accord with her own emotional state. She hovered by the side and assumed a space that she estimated would mark an invisible point on an invisible circumference surrounding where the group had gathered.

There was a sudden roar of battered clouds and severed sky. Someone else, who was standing on that invisible circumference, looked at her and pointed up at two planes.

"Fighter jets," he said, with a careful foot forward, inching in toward the group. He looked up and frowned a little. "Flying real low." The jets roared overhead. He shouted, "And loud!"

That's when the bus arrived. She thought it would be nice to sit on the bus together in silence with him, but there was room for everyone to sit alone.

The bus chugs toward a faint glimmering form ahead while it winds around the new road. This whole place used to be an airport: dead-flat seven hundred acres that hadn't been in use in thirty years.

The AllOver headquarters is round and glistening like an egg from a benevolent alien species. It is so stunning, so eye-catching, that at first glance, Teresa doesn't notice the old hangars tucked in the back. Each of them gutted and renovated inside, but the coarse exteriors remain the same. The rough texture of the hangars enhances the luster of the main structure. Crust with shine. A pearl to harvest. It is gorgeous at eye level but nowhere near the picture of futuristic tranquility that AllOver depicted in render images to court the locals back in 2014. Back when her father was alive. He thought it sounded like a good company and someone had to do something with that land. No commercial plot can stay unoccupied forever. It would have been this or a casino, probably, is what he said at the time.

Neighborhood blogs and local papers endlessly circulated the pictures that seemed more like space settlements, actual planets away from the typical new developments like strip malls and mid-market condominiums. They called it "Render Falls," a nickname that has stuck. Maybe it is because the word "render" was unfamiliar to the people in Stoughton until they saw the images. The word sounded technical and new, just like AllOver was, but the old Stuart Falls Memorial Airport had been an internet-to-physical-world portal too. Teenage drinkers and ruin porn spelunkers would scale the fence with old mattress toppers and thick carpets. They'd post pictures of its blighted eighties business-class splendor to image blogs and Tumblr. Among its decrepit peculiarities was a staircase covered at every step with stacks of ledgers, flight chart maps, spiral notebooks, and canvas binders. Documented at many angles, with various types of camera apps and filters, the spectacle resembled a waterfall of office supplies—the natural wonder that the airport was originally named for.

Alone in her row, Teresa pulls up the old render images on her phone and counts where the building comes up short. The hangars were razed in the architectural renderings. The render images are richly forested but there are no trees outside and their absence gives the grounds a look of industrial nakedness and severity. In the images, there are hundreds of people around, cut-and-pasted in like paper doll cutouts, active around the campus: crowding at picnic tables and throwing a Frisbee across the lawn. There's a rendered golden retriever with a red bandana running about off-leash. One of the paper-doll render men plays guitar. But there is no one outside her window. No trees and no people. There aren't even structures to accommodate people, like picnic tables or benches. The immaculate grass looks spiky, like it could pierce the soles of your shoes if you were to cross it, with or without a Frisbee. Spike grass—is that a thing? Spike glass? Maybe no one actually works here besides robots.

The shuttle bus slows as it turns into the receiving area. The building catches its white and green trim finish, colors that replicate in particles and swirl along its own surface. An interpretation of the vehicle flickers and darts through the iridescent glass panels, which otherwise reflect the hesitant color of the overcast sky. The shuttle parks at the opal mouth of Render Falls, while it continues to move in flickering reflections. Teresa is the last to get off, and on her way out, her foot catches in the rubber step pad. Her mangled confetti-speck mirror image splashes over the building that she is about to enter. She trips but lands on her feet and spins on her heels to balance. From where she stands, it is all spike grass and gray sky. Render Falls looks like anywhere there ever was.

Looking left, out in the distance, she notices odd trucks, heavy haulers, in a queue to enter a rickety old hangar. Each has a shiny, glinting carriage unit, pearlescent with stylized texture. The trucks remind her of the hermit crabs she had as a kid, their rough bodies like truck bodies. She had always loved picking out iridescent shells at the pet store; pretty new homes for the little weird creatures. The trucks look just as unsuitably matched with their pretty payload coverings. The place feels weird, but weird is not bad. This could be a good job, she thinks again, as she enters the spacious lobby.

They gather under an abstract bronze chandelier shaped like branches and daggers. The floor is marble, milky pink; the same color and glazed-donut opacity as the interior of the converted office in Marlborough where the AllOver pre-screening took place. Teresa had waited in the stiff chairs in the reception area, across from a teenager on her phone and two retirement-age men in scratched-up work boots and faded jeans. Half the walls were painted gray and the other half were covered in a trippy geode-pattern wallpaper. Everything else was pink.

A woman in a silver shift dress and a full face of makeup called for her and escorted her down the pink hallway. Bethany was her name. Six feet tall in patent leather beige heels. The conservative polish to the representative's attire was all the more striking and strange as she appeared to be no more than a year or two out of school. As they walked together down the hall, Teresa wondered about the spatial frame with narrow passages and closed doors nestled one after the next. It reminded her of a private practice of some kind of medical specialist. When they entered a tiny room and Bethany closed the door, Teresa half expected to change into a smock and step in stirrups. Instead of an examination table, the room's centerpiece was another cumbersome device, unfamiliar to her but evidently designed to receive a full body just the same. It was dark red and slanted from a helmet with telephone cord–like tight spirals that connected to arm straps and two halves of metal and fabric to wrap across each leg. Bethany strapped her in and snapped the visor over her eyes. Through the visor, Teresa could see a digital environment, a picture of this room but sharper; real almost, but crisp at the object edges. The illusion died at those edges.

"Don't overthink it," Bethany said. "This is only a baseline reflex and hand-eye coordination test. There is nothing to win." Teresa was transported from the geode wallpaper to a virtual endless expanse of AllOver pink. The digital environment was shadowless and looked slick, like flatlands covered in strawberry milk.

"Jump over the rings and catch each ball."

Teresa, startled by Bethany's instructions, crouched at her core and loosened her shoulders to prepare for the test. Tennis balls, rendered in impressive detail, shot out to her from the strawberry-milk vanishing point. She snatched at the air with loose fists. The rendered objects evaporated with each successful catch. Teresa was surprised at how easy the test was—maybe she was a natural; even when the tennis balls accelerated and faked out, she was ready. The rings were rings of fire—a facsimile, considerably less lifelike than in the previous task. What the rendering lacked in photorealism, it made up for in aggression. The fire rings thrusted toward her feet in sharklike baited zigzags. A ring charged at her and she jumped up. A success. She could dodge the rings easily, even while she ethered the virtual tennis balls. When the balls and rings vanished into the pastel void, Bethany said she did great and told her where to meet for the shuttle the following week.

They check in with a dark-haired woman at the front desk—nearly identical to Bethany from the pre-screening—who collects their phones and stores them individually in a card catalog–style cabinet. Each little drawer is lined with pink satin to match the floors; the flash of color looks teasing and out of place, like a display case at an upmarket lingerie shop. Some of the trainees brought laptops, which she secures in a lockbox under her desk. Teresa remembers how proud she was locking up the cash and diamond rings in the safe at Cedars that time years ago but not a mile away. Maybe this will be a good job. Crawling up the sides of the wall are cold silver geranium-style flowers snaking their way through vents in a chrome divider. Silver flowers. Metallic flowers. The flowers must be synthetic, but the green leaves and vines look alive.

"Teresa Kelly," she says. The woman at the front desk scans for her name on the tablet interface. "AO. Stoughton, CR" is embossed on the front of the desk under the

AllOver logo. Teresa wonders about it. Shouldn't it say, "Stoughton, MA"?

She catches the name of the person she was talking to earlier: Al Jin. She notices his hand clutches something in his back pocket after he checks in. Has he held on to his phone? Teresa wonders. She smiles, but he's looking out at the spike grass through the window.

Before the group is a harried-looking man with flushed skin and pale clothes that suggest an unidentifiable spring vegetable in a CSA basket. He ducks slightly when he enters the lobby, although the doorframe has half a foot on him. Philip is his name. He offers a tight wave to the crowd and walks past the woman at the front desk without saying anything more. Teresa, at this angle, can see his face contort into a grimace in profile.

They follow Philip down a white corridor. It is clean and it smells of packed dust like the inside of a vacuum. It sounds like compressed air: nothingness with volume, noise-canceling acoustics at super strength exerting a deafening void. The sound of their steps through the hall—fifty-one pairs of feet—dissolves in the overpowering silence.

Through silver sliding doors, they arrive at Turing Hall, the name of one of the old hangars. The floors are painted with white resin. Traffic cones segment a quarter of the space where the group will be working. The other sections of the old hangar are white nothing under ceilings taller than airplanes with exposed joists. In the back, there's a long table with a breakfast buffet: pans of pancakes, bacon, hash browns, and fruit; tea and coffee in silver urns by a tower of mugs; and trays of muffins and other pastries. A nice spread. The kind of breakfast that conferencing executives might expect, not contract workers solicited off Craigslist. Teresa fills her plate with melon and peanut butter on a tiny bagel. It will be a good job, she wants to believe. She has a cup of coffee quickly and refills the cup before taking a seat in one of the electric blue foldout chairs lined up in the center of the space.

"Welcome to AllOver. The experience company," Philip begins. His voice is amplified by a hidden mic. "Our mission is to connect customers and entertainment and service providers, to empower businesses and content creators to maximize their success, and to make person-to-person experiences and exchanges universally accessible, progressive, and equitable."

He glances at his notes with a look of practiced solemnity. "Today's training is held in a sacred place that is traditional Sakimauchheen Ing and Algonquin soil," he says, quick and mumbly, sure to have mispronounced it. All of AllOver's meetings and public events begin with a land acknowledgment but Philip has got this one wrong. He had failed to refresh the TribalLandz app on his phone and announced the origin of the suburbs of Philadelphia, which was the last place that he had hosted a training session. Otherwise, he would have said it was Wampanoag territory.

"Everyone in this room has a role to play to make this future our reality. You're the first New England division of AllOver's brand-new CR program."

Those letters again. Initials? No, it doesn't seem like it, Teresa thinks. She stares at the letters on the screen behind Philip as she would a pair of Scrabble tiles. Ah. "Car" without a vowel. They will be driving after all.

3

AllOver was founded in 2012, Philip tells the crowd as Teresa picks at the last of her cantaloupe. Muddled daylight washes in through the skylight panels and catches his stringy vegetable hair in a backscatter orb of glow. "If the company were a baby, he'd get behind the wheels this year.

"AllOver is more than a service and experience platform. It's about community," Philip continues. "We bridge humanity and enterprise; we shape the digital economy to fit neighborhood-centric needs. AllOver is personal and it is social. Everyone in this room has an account but no two people have the same adventures with our services. Maybe you're a gamer or you love to travel or order Ethiopian takeout through our app. As a company, we are large, but the connections we offer are intimate and special. Half of all our eight hundred million users have completed a transaction through our platform today. Eighty-seven percent of service-based small businesses route bookings with our calendar and transaction stack. We're a network of hardworking people united to build a future that benefits us all." The more he speaks, the more his words seem charged with bitter enthusiasm; a grinding attempt at cheer that grows more pronounced as he compliments the room for fulfilling two of AllOver's values in hiring: racial diversity and an equal number of women and men. "I see we got a lot of Libras in this room," he says with a smile that doesn't look fake. "Good energy."

"No vehicle needed and no driving experience necessary" is all the Craigslist ad had said. Her phone rang an hour after she fired off an email in response. Normally, she'd attach a résumé and cover letter, but she had intuited, given the brevity of the "Drivers Wanted" ad, that it was in her best interest to respond to it in a quick and casual manner similar to how it was written.

The recruiter described the position in a vague way that made her feel like she had been plucked for an apprenticeship in wheelwrighting or stone masonry but for this century and into the next one. Eight weeks of paid training. There was something appealing about the opportunity to be "trained"; she'd be an expert in something. There would be a clear beginning and an end and after that end a new beginning.

"This is one of our finest clients. I imagine you are familiar with AllOver," the recruiter said on the phone. A male voice, boldly intoned, he sounded proud of her—this stranger—like she'd won a prize. The company had already conducted a thorough background check on her, which she aced, the recruiter said. Teresa paused to consider the legality of this. AllOver must have scanned their own data. They would know all the airline flights that she had ever taken and every movie theater ticket she had purchased for well over a decade. Every subway ride and museum admission, every haircut and Pilates class. That time she went to Six Flags with former co-workers at an office where she had been temping. She had used AllOver autopay to send her rent directly to her old roommate with his name on the lease. Her YMCA membership had been paid each month in AllCash points. Even her cobbler on Huntington, a shop that's been in business since 1823, processed her payments with AllOver. What would his great-great-grandfather say? They'd know she's lived in two states. Unmarried. She once had a dog. They'd know this because she had paid the walker with AllOver and the kennel fees too. They'd have her old Brookline address, her older addresses in Forest Hills and Hyde Park, other addresses in New York, a brief stint back in Stoughton, and the street she lives on now in Brixboro. Teresa, reluctantly, in spite of herself, felt a dash of pride. AllOver could see a substantial part of her life history and they thought she looked okay.

"This is a worker-first company. You'll be in good hands," the recruiter continued. AllOver combined efficient logistics with consumer-oriented design and customer service. "There's an ethics board; *Fortune* magazine ranked it the best Silicon Valley company for diversity, equity, and inclusion; and *Barron's* called it the world's most sustainable corporate enterprise. Its staff is unionized. This is a contract position, no benefits, but that's how everyone gets their foot in the door these days," he said.

"Could you tell me what a typical day might entail?" Teresa asked, holding her cellphone close to her mouth, worried the recruiter might otherwise hear the floorboard creaking or the window rattling, as it does whenever cars drive on the rural town road she lives on. The house had belonged to an unmarried great-aunt who left it to her mother. That relative had passed away shortly after her father. The timing was fortuitous despite another layer of grief: her mother, at that time, was facing eviction from the house Teresa grew up in.

Teresa worried the recruiter would ask what she was doing in Brixboro or what the town was like. "There's a rail trail. I like to go there for a run" was what she might have said, and it's true, on weekends when it's nice, she'll go for a sprint on the old railway corridor, now a thin strip of packed dirt along the brook tented with the branches of maple trees and white pine. Also, there's a beautiful library made of stone with the year 1843 chiseled in the rounded arch above the doors. The rooms are drafty in the winter, but in this weather it is a good place to work on job applications with a robust Wi-Fi connection. Teresa thought she would stay here three months. Then the gaps between jobs lengthened and her hourly rate stagnated and now it has been over a year. Brixboro is less than ideal, but she could say the same for anywhere she's lived.

"That's a billion-dollar question," the recruiter laughed. "Before I get ahead of myself, you said in the application that you love to drive?"

"Yes, I love to. So this is something like Uber, right?"

"Nothing like that," he laughed again. "Uber was twentieth-century logistics and prewar infrastructure paired with a smartphone app interface. It was old news inside start-up gift-wrapping and VC investment icing the cake. This is not a cake. It is entirely new." Training's twenty-five dollars an hour, he said. "Not bad, and there's a job guarantee." Workers will have tremendous flexibility in hours and can expect a grand a week in take-home pay as soon as training ends. "I can't tell you what it is, but I just know that before long it's going to be a job that everyone wants. Look, I might be calling you for work a few years down the road."

Teresa was flattered and skeptical at once.

"Consider it this way: you are getting paid to learn a trade that, to the rest of the world, hasn't been invented yet," he said. "You're a VIP with a backstage pass to a new career. Now are you in?"

She was. Whatever it is, the job is already better than her last five LinkedIn updates. Most of that work happened in mills: old mill yards, old gristmills, old leather mills, old textile mills. Sometimes they were called that. Woolen Mills was one of her old offices but abstracted from its original purpose in time and determination. The name of the brick building reminded her of owl eyes with the duplicate Os looking down at her from the sign at the front entrance. At least two of her former offices were called "The Old Mill." Long rigid brick towers sturdy enough to support manufacturing purposes. Each one renovated inside to edgy modern plainness. Some had working water mills on-site. Even in the not-so-great jobs, she enjoyed the sounds of slush and grind in the forecourts of those odd buildings. Sometimes the hallways were decorated with tarnished old equipment made of wheels, levers, bells, and mesh buckets. At a short data-entry post, she had a desk behind the floor showpiece: an old contraption that looked like an ancient birdcage topped with a Brannock Device. Another mill had an eleven-foot-tall power loom wheel on display in the hall. All of the mills had history. Her temporary coworker at a 3D-printing start-up in Lawrence casually mentioned to her that the Bread and Roses Strike happened at that mill more than a hundred years ago. She never saw him again after that. His contract must have ended.

Teresa used to drive to these jobs in her mother's beige Impreza with a weak FM signal and the AC busted. She would hang her blouse on the headrest of the passenger seat, safe from wrinkles and sweat, and navigate that clunker in a camisole and office attire from the waist down. The windows rolled open, her hair in tendrils flopping across her face, she'd listen to the putt-putt sputter of the old motor on her way to whatever address was listed on the latest guest badge lanyard in the cupholder. Crackle- and static-distorted rock songs from the twentieth century wheezing out from the stereo until she found a spot in the parking lot of whichever mill she was working out of that day.

Some of the mills were almost beautiful inside when the sun hit through the lake-size windows built at a time when a workday depended on natural light.

Inside every office were rows of people dressed in stiff patterned shirts looking at screens. She'd glance over the shoulders of the young women reading articles in the *Harvard Business Review* about the struggles women faced in the workforce or she'd notice the middle-aged men on Facebook arguing with their family about *New York Times* op-eds. She would envy them and wonder if she would ever feel comfortable enough, hired enough, reliably employed enough to scroll through rain boots on Amazon on one window while entering numbers into a spreadsheet with a ten-key in a dual-screen setup. Such idle internet time-wasting was for the permanent staff, and she was always there to work with an exit date predetermined.

Like an actor's stand-in, Teresa typically filled a gap left by someone else. Parental leave was the most common reason. At every place, they'd make the same joke on her first day: "You're the new Jessica!" For shorter assignments, she'd step in for someone away on vacation, like an accountant's receptionist in Billerica and the front-desk person who signed for packages—that seemed to be all the job was, signing for packages—at a freight-forwarding company in Framingham. Once she was sent to conduct user testing for the website of a renewable-energy start-up inside the massive old textile mill complex in Maynard. A man in a blazer and jeans with deep circles under his eyes walked over to her empty desk and said, "We'll have that laptop ready for you soon. Just sit tight." She waited alone in a cubicle for eight hours each day with nothing to do. He signed her timesheet on Friday and said the company no longer needed her. Most of the time she wasn't in an office at all. She was looking and calling and emailing for somewhere to be. For the past decade, it had felt like her job had been the waiting. The work was the easy part.

Teresa loved to drive. She wasn't just saying it to get the job. When she came upon the Craigslist post, she had spent the afternoon, as she typically would, sending out her résumé for various low-rung office positions. "Drivers wanted." It called out to her. She would have ignored it, perhaps, on any other day, but on that one, she considered it: What is more ordinary and freeing than the driver's seat, courting destiny with your right heel? She felt, when she composed the email to the recruiter, a strong desire for the independence of the road, like how a teenager with a learner's permit imagines their near future. Also, she was grounded. Well, as grounded as a woman her age could be.

"I don't want you taking the Impreza anymore," her mother had said last month, as she cracked a fistful of dry spaghetti in half and threw it in a boiling pot. "It's okay to take it around town but with the mileage you've been putting in, no. Take the bus."

"How am I supposed to get to work?" Teresa had just come back from the library. She noticed an incomprehensible stew of apples and tomatoes that her mother had boiling in another pot. There was only a ceiling fan to counter the summer humidity. Teresa grabbed a junk mail postcard and fanned herself. "It's half an hour to the commuter rail alone and those tickets are expensive." Another hour to Boston, she calculated in her head. What would that be, three hours to Quincy, at least. "I don't have any say in it if my next contract is in Taunton or someplace real far. I am trying to save for a place already. I can't afford a new car too."

"If it breaks down, we've got nothing," her mother

said. And that was it. They sat together in Teresa's room—momentarily a living room—and watched baking shows on television. Her mother nibbled on her weird stew. Teresa ate some of the pasta with feta and lettuce. It was fine. Empty bowls, forks, and napkins collected on the side table where Teresa leaves her reading glasses and charges her phone at night. After her mother went to bed, Teresa took the dishes to the sink. She pulled the neatly folded blanket from the sofa, which is actually a daybed—her bed. And that night, like every night, she fell asleep as all her mental energy compiled to conjure up one thought: how much she despises the place that she's in—this state of existence, this everything. She concentrates on this anti-desire, only to let it go and forget it until the next night.

Teresa couldn't drive to Render Falls anyway. No outside vehicles are allowed, not even bikes. It had something to do with security. Robots don't drive after all, and this wasn't a space for humans.

She never asked the recruiter why they didn't allow cars in the Render Falls lot, but if she could, and if she had access to that Impreza still, Teresa would curve down Route 128 each morning from Brixboro to Stoughton, from west of Boston to the South Shore. Years ago, the region was the nation's technology hub, home to microprocessor and semiconductor companies, back when tech company names ended with the words "Electronics" and "Incorporated." After the war, well after the mills were decommissioned, defense contracting money flooded into Boston's northwest and west suburbs. Some of the mills became offices, and pig farms were paved over for industrial parks all along this "highway to nowhere," which circled around but never crossed Boston and only barely touched the region south. If you bought a minicomputer from a company with a name like Micro-CompSystemsCorpInc, well, it probably came from a team that worked somewhere in this part of the state. By the 1990s, the companies went bankrupt or were bought out by Silicon Valley victors. They were scrappier out west, ex-hippie workaholics, who had their minds altered with LSD and combined that with gearheadedness. The Massachusetts computer scientists wore ties, went to church, had families, and prioritized their weekends. They accepted the world as it was and lacked the selfish passion that e-commerce demanded of them.

Stoughton is where she grew up, and now she has returned in a way. If only she could take a direct trip through this fallow landscape: through highways and wealthy towns, mansions and business parks in clean terra-cotta brick with no ornament or mill history, past the gas stations and Portuguese bakeries. From the highways, all you can see are rolling golden fields that will be reduced to pavement and more industrial parks eventually with the next wave of something: clean energy, gene editing, any idea that can be harnessed for profit by ordinary-looking people with homes and offices and lives that plot on a map, easily.

4

The trainees sit quietly in Turing Hall as an enormous screen lowers from the ceiling. Electronic music pipes through the speakers and a fractal animation plays before a cut to Falconer Guidry, the founder and CEO of AllOver, in close-up.

"My mother always said that to be the best you have to work the hardest. But what I tell my kids is that there's no value in being the best if you can't lift everyone up to your level." He's lean and healthy in appearance with a pinched face and a look of perpetual surprise due to his unusually high eyebrows.

"What we have at AllOver is a culture of success that comes from every one of us. I call it the 'Holistic Apex.'"

Teresa recognizes the words as the title of his new book. A tower of copies is stacked in the window display at Jimmy's Newsstand in South Station. Bullet points appear on-screen as he elaborates. "Holistic Apex" is a "working philosophy of humanism for collaboratively superb achievement." Among its central tenets is a commitment to AI for good, "purposeful" data collection, sustainability, and technology "used sparingly and only in the service of human dignity."

"Winning means everyone wins," Falconer says, as the words appear next to him on-screen in an airy typeface. "Our future is to be shared. Every single human life is priceless; our humanity will never be duplicated, not with the intelligence of a hundred thousand machines." He ends with a brief overview of an upcoming pilot program providing a universal basic income to AllOver staff around the globe. It is scheduled to begin in the next calendar year and available to any full-time and permanent staff member. There's a quick montage of AllOver in the news. *Forbes* magazine ranked it the eighth most trusted company in America. *Fortune* magazine says it has the best diversity, equity, and inclusion policies. Teresa remembers the recruiter praising this on the phone just the same.

The video cuts to footage of Falconer meeting with janitors and cafeteria workers at their Redwood City headquarters. "We believe in excellence from the bottom-up," Falconer says, patting the shoulder of one of the cooks, who holds a cane in one hand and a leash in the other. Falconer leans down to scratch the ears of the worker's service dog. "Even this good boy is part of our apex. Aren't you, bud?"

Something is off about Falconer's delivery. He tangles each long vowel and pauses after every clause. The effect is calming but disorienting. He's crispy on the sides, like those virtual reality environments she encountered in the pre-screening. That and the equipoise to his eyebrows. Teresa wonders if it's Falconer at all or a CGI animation of his likeness.

The video cuts to more fractals and geometric animations. Needles and quartz shapes cascade across the screen like pickup sticks and merge to form the company logo with geode slices for the "A" and the "O." A woman with a BBC British accent takes over to narrate the history of the company over a montage of maps and footage of teams of happy AllOver employees at offices around the world: Dublin, Singapore, Bogotá, Nairobi, and Rome.

"From an early age, Falconer Guidry could draw insights and explore the potential of curated, structured, and assorted data," the narrator says as the video cuts to a snapshot of a chart he drew as a nine-year-old that plotted the likelihood for each day of the week that his next baby teeth would fall out. "In every second, a quarter of the land on earth is transmitting a request through AllOver. It is AllOver the world that we come together and provide. It is the highest honor that we get to share the apex with you. We welcome you aboard our next great experiment."

Teresa turns around, to get a sense of the space and the crowd. Sitting near her is a woman with frizzy aubergine hair and a well-worn tote bag looped over her chair that reads, "And She Who Gives the Least F*cks Wins." The asterisk in place of a "u" makes the word look more impudent. Her name is Maryvonne but Teresa hasn't learned it yet. For now, Teresa knows her as "She Who Gives the Least F*cks."

The woman from the front desk—or another AllOver staffer who looks just like her—walks over to She Who Gives the Least F*cks and taps her on the shoulder. "Right this way," she whispers. The trainee nods. They leave quietly while the video continues.

On-screen is an aerial shot of the AllOver headquarters: it looks like an even bigger alien egg than the place they are currently stationed in. The video pans in at the curb, where a giant podlike vehicle in electric blue—the same color as the folding chairs—appears. It has round headlights and a grille with upturned corners, which gives the bubble-like vehicle the appearance of a smiling face.

"No driver. All machine. All intuition. Sterile excellence. Out on the open road, it offers you an unparalleled respite. Absolute privacy matched with the ultimate passenger experience," announces the disembodied BBC voice.

A woman, ballerina-thin and tall, exits one of the blue pods on-screen. Her ash-blond hair is combed back in a dense pompadour. She wears a white crepe dress, loose at the waist, and around her wrists and neck are heavy Viking-style silver cuffs. Teresa wonders if it was she who picked out the aggressive chandelier in the foyer. The words "Vermont Qualline, SVP automotive engineering" appear in overlay text as the woman pats the vehicle below the windshield as if it were alive, like an obedient pet.

On-screen is yet another montage set to electronic music as Vermont Qualline tours their regional office in Rio Rancho, New Mexico. At this alien egg in the desert, a team of three hundred designers and engineers "worked in secret" to perfect driverless-vehicle technology. "Now have a look inside," she says, pointing to four swivel seats in mushroom beige leather. Arne Jacobsen's Egg chair appears to have inspired the designers, as the seats contour roundly and inward. There is something primordial about the shape—the seats don't look cozy, exactly, but each appears ready to hug a passenger in place. Vermont returns to her seat in the CR and Teresa recognizes the woman's tidy, dovelike face. She is the daughter of George "Honey Q" Qualline, the country singer with that crossover hit song from the nineties, "Good Enough Is Still Good." Vermont used to be in teen movies. She modeled in the Cedars catalog and there was a poster of her on the wall by the juniors section dressing rooms when Teresa worked there. Whenever Teresa went to the back closet to swap out music videos, she would see her, posing in some kind of bandeau-and-miniskirt getup. Sometimes Teresa wondered, when she'd rewind the VHS tapes and look at Vermont's perfectly symmetrical face, what it must be like to have a life that is easy. Vermont's elegant hair color might be natural gray. Her grace and imposing stylishness—not beauty, exactly, but the fidelity to first-class grooming that has a similar disarming impact—gives Teresa an occasion to envy the celebrity-stranger once again.

"You might ask, why driverless? Why now?" The camera pans out on Falconer to reveal he's sitting at a kitchen table with an old woman. "Because my grandmother can't drive anymore. I knew I had to build a safe way for her to get to the grocery store."

Not a bad reason, Teresa thinks. But what's in it for us?

5

W ell, that seems incredibly unlikely," says the trainee sitting next to Teresa. "But at least the animations were entertaining."

"What do you mean?" The video has ended, and a few people have left their seats to grab more coffee.

"Those cars don't work the way they're saying." He shakes his head and laughs. "Remember when self-driving cars were all over the news for a while and then nothing happened? You got things like light rail kind of systems out west. They go on planned routes to avoid cracked-up streets, but as soon as it rains, forget it. My sister lives in Oakland. She told me that people used to shoot pocket lasers out their windows to trick them. The cars would stop because they'd think it's a red light."

"That's really funny."

"Now how is AllOver about to take these cars around

the rotaries in Boston? And with all the potholes, no way. We'll be safety drivers, is my guess, but actually driving most of the time."

"Safety drivers." Teresa tries to picture this. Maybe one of the seats inside swivels around, but it didn't look like it.

"That's my guess. The name's Ken." He's one of the youngest trainees in the room, about twenty-six years old.

Ken looks back at the screen, now blank and bright. "What I don't understand is how we'll fit in those cars with the passengers and how the seats are set up. Where is the steering wheel? The car in the demo was probably just for show. We'll be driving in something a lot less cool-looking, probably."

"Yeah, I don't know," Teresa says. She senses he'd like her to say something cynical about the demo they watched, but for as corny as it might have been, she doesn't want to screw things up with this job. At least not yet.

Teresa makes her way back to the snack tray. It's another great spread. Sandwiches, fruit and cheese, petit fours, more coffee and tea. "How old are yours?" she overhears Abril ask Nichelle. Abril has two boys at home, six and eight. She was caring for her mother, who passed away; got back together with her high school boyfriend, but after the second kid, he split. Teresa glances over Nichelle's shoulder. There is Al Jin by the orange cones, away from the crowd, rustling with something in his pocket again. He looks around, but he does not check behind him, where Teresa stands. She's listening to Abril and Nichelle, sort of, and wonders if it makes sense for her to move back to Stoughton. Or Quincy, which might feel considerably less strange. A studio or a furnished basement; at the very least, a proper bedroom. Privacy. Time to herself and time to think. Now Abril's talking about her new boyfriend, who coaches her sons' soccer league. "Sounds nice," Teresa says, nodding her head, trying to appear that she had been paying attention to the conversation more closely than she had been.

Back in the blue chairs, there's another video presentation, a preview of the commercial scheduled to announce the CR program this winter. It features Plum Sasha, the teenage influencer, icy-looking, like a young Vermont Qualline in a shorter skirt. Plum sits at the counter of an old-fashioned soda fountain and sips a chocolate egg cream from a tulip glass. She has on a jean dress and a gaudy tiara, which looks strange, but Teresa read somewhere that tiaras are the latest teen fashion trend. Plum pulls out her phone and taps a silver-and-blue icon. A CR pod pulls up to the curb. She jumps in—all rowdy smiles, like she's piled into the back seat of a friend's car before a joyride. Plum punches the ceiling of the CR and a screen pops down. The leather seats grip into her thighs as she focuses on a first-person shooter game. There is a mix of time-lapse footage out the window: downtown Los Angeles morphs into Pacific Ocean vistas and finally, in drone footage, the globular blue car triumphantly crosses the Golden Gate Bridge. The CR stops in front of the Painted Ladies houses. Plum exits the vehicle and runs out to join a group of young people lazing on blankets in the park. "Los Angeles to the Bay Area in six hours tops. Only two hundred bucks flat. It's a trip out of town. Not a trip to the bank," she says with a big grin. Plum turns back to join the crowd. The commercial ends.

Philip returns to the front of the room. "So that is a CR. Now back to CR . . . ed! You know, like driver's ed? CR ed. Okay, tough crowd." He bites into an apple and the sound of the chomp reverberates through space.

Ken raises his hand. "What's it stand for? CR, I mean."

Philip looks surprised. "Just like a car, I guess. But they changed the pronunciation a few months back because it got a little confusing talking about the 'car program' and the 'car service.' Plus, it's more than just a car. The CR is a lifestyle."

Ken looks over the image of the CR on the screen. "So it's a shuttle service?"

"No, no. People don't like to share cars. That's why Uber Pool failed." There's no plan for an introductory flat rate out of Boston as of yet, he continues, but should they implement the "Longcar CR" plan to New York or DC it might be even less—$150, $100.

"No kidding," Abril says, nodding her head cautiously. "I'd go for that."

"Right? Anyone would. These are Amtrak prices, but this is like your own private Amtrak. And it's clean. This is as clean as transportation gets, with fresh air ventilated with premium HEPA purifiers. Have you been on the subway around here? The seats are dirty, the poles are gross. People cough and sneeze and chew their smelly food right next to you. You get gum on your shoes. Who wants that? AllOver is providing an economical and comfortable transportation alternative for customers to live their best lives as they journey from one part of the city to another."

Someone in the back row asks if people might use them for overnights, like couchettes in those fancy trains they got overseas.

"No bathroom," Philip says, frowning. "But next year, two years, who knows?" The prices are limited time only. For now, the program is exclusive for "Rose Quartz" AllOver customers, the top 5 percent active users of All-Over products and services each year. The hangar falls silent. In this extended pause, the trainees all focus their attention on the image of the blue car paused on the screen. Here it is: a tomorrow, previewed just for them. A new departure, a brand-new implementation, a beacon of something. A future that will happen somehow and someway, and a future that asked them to participate.

Ken raises his hand again. "If these cars drive themselves, then why are we here?"

"Great question." Philip doesn't answer it. "What's it

like inside? Well, you sit back, stream some Netflix, and before you know it, you're in the Back Bay. You're in Fenway Paaaaahk! Hold on, keep going, okay, now you're cruising into the Wang Theatre. Just in time for the next matinee performance of *Hamilton*. No traffic to stress you out. You can even take a little nap in the neatest, cleanest vehicle before you get there. This isn't just a car; it's a shortcut to a better life."

Ken stands up so the room can hear him. "So we're safety drivers. I couldn't see a space inside the car for us to sit."

"Kind of," Philip says. "It's more challenging and a lot more fun than that. All those self-driving car crashes you used to hear about? Safety drivers got bored. Customers aren't safe if you're bored. You aren't safe if you get bored. You won't get bored, I promise you that."

Ken, in the row ahead of her on the bus, has turned around and handed her his phone. "Here. Check this out."

The YouTube video on his screen says, "Self Driving Tesla Drives Its Owner To Work & Then Finds A Parking Spot." She takes one of his earbuds and listens. "Paint It Black" blasts over footage, front-facing, of a car dashboard and view through the windshield. A man has his hands cupped under the steering wheel without touching it. The steering wheel turns with smooth motion as the car takes a left onto a minimally trafficked road, before moving on to a highway and returning to the suburban street. The man in the driver's seat has his hands folded in his lap; all the while the wheel keeps turning.

"What do you think?"

Teresa's confused. Didn't Ken just tell her the cars don't work? "I didn't know they were so advanced," she says.

Ken shakes his head. "That video was shot over four days. They drove five hundred miles. Elon had it edited down to three minutes. It's like if I filmed myself jumping up and down and cut all the footage of my feet on the ground and said, 'Here's proof I can levitate.' No one scams like that if they ever plan to build."

The bus is moving north against the traffic on Route 93. Outside the window, the sky is cloudy over the rainbow-painted gas tank before Savin Hill Beach.

"Do you hear him say 'top five percent active users'?" The bus has slowed to a snail's pace on the expressway and she can hear Ken's words clearer without the friction of gusts of wind batting at the windows. "Has to be the top five percent who spend the most money. What kind of bottom-up change begins with people who spend fifty gs or so on an app every year?"

Arriving at South Station, the trainees depart with no goodbyes. Teresa boards the commuter rail and transfers to the Brixboro bus in Framingham. Her mind is still and aerated, like breeze through a house with all the windows open. It is raining outside and it is dark. Red brake lights from the cars ahead are reflected in the wet pavement like lipstick scrawled on a mirror. The job could be good. There's at least one good thing about this job, Teresa thinks: it gets her out of the house.

6

This could be the worst commute she's had in terms of time and distance, but Teresa comes to love it. She can sleep on the bus to Framingham, that's easy; and when she arrives at the commuter rail platform, there comes a warm feeling that she's reentered society. All the people together with their clean work clothes, laptops, and coffees; with their solemn faces and solitude in public. The older women with reading glasses on a chain and the men in ties with ink-stained fingertips after thumbing through newspapers. The young workers who might be living with their parents, like she is, and saving up for a place closer to the city. And the slightly older young workers who could only afford houses out this way. Everyone alone and bundled together, on a journey for the same thing that is to be found in different places—all the offices, somewhere in or around Boston. She likes the feeling that she is one of them. She's just another body on the train; there is a place she needs to be.

It is an elegant ride, smooth and effortless motion, whipping past the towns with duck ponds and colonial estates while the darkness lifts in increments. At each stop, the sky is lighter, the passengers get older. The shoes get nicer when the train gets closer to the city, and the passengers are more likely to carry briefcases and Sundry Meadows coffees.

The train arrives at South Station and her day has begun. She feels like a party has ended, momentarily, while there is another whirl of train station–people traffic. There are crowds and more crowds from the platform to the main hall; scattered crowds, not one person is with another person. People tend to spend their mornings alone.

Teresa finds an angle around an attendant standing in the center of the station and dashes to the queue for the restroom. At the mirror farthest from the door is a woman with frosted hair with all her belongings strewn around one of the sinks. She burrows through her makeup kit with clawlike, small, twitchy hands. The entire restroom smells like musty chalk. The old talcum scent makes Teresa think of the eighties. The powders are ancient or oxidized, probably teeming with bacteria. While not fully wretched, it smells like nothing a person would want on their face.

Stepping forward with the queue, Teresa can see the woman's shattered compacts of fuchsia blusher, crumbly remnants of eyeshadow palettes, and eye pencils sharpened to the wick scattered from the faucet to the border tiles. There's a trail of purple metallic substance from the sink to a puddle on the floor. Teresa finds a clean stall, and when she steps back out, the only sink available is the one that is next to the woman with the makeup spilling all over. She's twitching hard now as she applies mascara in poppyseed clumps. Teresa washes her hands thoroughly and it occurs to her that the woman with the makeup must be down on her luck. The woman does not have a place to be—she is not like the train passengers, she's not like Teresa.

"Stop watching me," says the stranger in a raspy voice. Teresa feels like a judgmental jerk, and to this poor woman, who is probably unhoused. On her way out, Teresa hears a jingle and a tap of heavy plastic. It is the sound of an object sturdier than a makeup compact. Teresa looks back at the woman, burrowing through her makeup once more. The woman retrieves a crusty makeup brush from her bag and grabs for keys on a ring with a Toyota key fob. Her twitchy, tiny motions remind Teresa of She Who Gives the Least F*cks.

The CR trainees are beginning to get to know one another. Outside South Station, Teresa joins Abril and Nichelle, familiar faces, but not yet friends. They gather in a haphazard circle between familiar strangers in line for the shuttle and the strangers with duffel bags and suitcases on their way to various platforms and exits.

Abril nods her head forward. "So what's this really about?"

"We're remote driving, is what I suspect. Like drone pilots," Nichelle says. "You know, they'll set us all up in a call center situation. Instead of phones, we'll get steering wheels and accelerator pedals."

"See, I don't think that's it," Abril says. "They could outsource, offshore all that."

"Could be a legal thing," Nichelle says. "Someone in the Philippines doesn't have a US driver's license. You saw those offices in the video, right? Why would they pay us decent for work that can be done in Quezon City? Benga-luru? My other guess is it has something to do with the tax code. I mean, I don't know what exactly. But every decision these companies make, it always comes down to money."

"Maybe we drive backup vehicles if there's a system-wide breakdown or something like that." Abril puts out her cigarette and grabs a bottle of water from her purse. "Or we spy on the passengers. Monitor every presence. Watch the floor with surveillance cameras to check that no one's shitting or fucking in there."

Monitoring passengers would be unpleasant, Teresa thinks. Although, at that hourly rate, she still wouldn't pass on the assignment. "But they asked for drivers, specifically."

Nichelle looks at Teresa and nods. "Drone pilot–style does seem most likely. But how would that even work? What if the system freezes up? Will the car crash if the internet goes down?"

"Glad I'm not the only one who is confused," Teresa says. "They aren't even giving us hints."

"My other guess is it's a prank. The secret cameras are on us. Some deranged billionaire gets off on getting unemployed people's hopes up," Abril says, with a tense look out to the curb. "I mean, what's with all the metaverse shit?"

Earlier that week, they met in Lovelace Studio, an open room divided into cubicles with white veils on stilts like a makeshift hospital. The trainees wore VR headsets and rested over foam semicircle blocks, knees to the floor and arms out like swimmers. They coursed through photoreal 360 images, first a picturesque Mediterranean beach town with multicolor buildings fit snug like decaying Tetris blocks leveling up over golden cliffs. Rickety fishing boats undulated in the azure sea. Other images looked like European cities in the rain, Paris or Amsterdam or Hamburg, somewhere Teresa has never been without a helmet. Between each virtual environment was a five-minute break, but rather than being restful, these intervals induced a sense of vertigo, which only gradually dissipated. Teresa felt her body and mind untether at her eyes; after the first hour, the exercises felt like climbing flights of stairs after a week with no sleep. By the end of the day, Teresa stalled out in the facsimile Big Sur Coast Highway just to rest her arms for a minute. She was glad that the animation paused, because if the hiccuping motion of the off-course animated car corresponded with reality in any way, she would have fallen off the cliff.

Ken wasn't in that session. He hasn't shown up for training since Monday.

"He quit," Abril says.

"How do you know?" Teresa asks.

"What's there to know? This is mandatory training and he's skipped out on three days."

"Where do you think they take Maryvonne?" Nichelle asks before the next shuttle pulls up to the curb.

"Is that her name? I don't know. I figured she was hired for a different kind of project that trains at the same time. But that's the other thing I wonder. When do they split us up? You can't drive as a team of fifty people."

Abril's comment leaves Teresa with a preposterous mental image of all the trainees driving tiny vehicles connected together with octopus-like arms. Driving an octopus. It's as unlikely as self-driving vehicles used to be.

There are eight Bethanys in Turing Hall. At least. There's Bethany Two from the front desk, who leads half the remaining forty-eight trainees to form a queue by the exit. Bethany Three rounds up the other half by the blue foldout chairs. The other six young women materialized in the staff corridor alongside Philip at breakfast. They never give their names. Then again, Teresa can't seem to recall how she learned the name of the first Bethany. Maybe she said something like "turn left with me" in a soft voice and Teresa misheard her. She feels somewhat guilty about being judgmental of them, but it is weird how they're all styled to look identical. There's some variation to their faces, but their figures, glossy blowout hair styles, wide eyes, and heavy layer of foundation are the same. Even the graceful way they move and gesture appears eerily synchronized. They might be automatons, but Teresa suspects the reality is more unsettling: someone in charge acted upon predilection.

Four women—or robots, a possibility she hasn't completely ruled out—organize Teresa's section into pairs. Trainees sit opposite each other at a card table with a chessboard between them.

"We play?" Ricardo asks.

"If you'd like," one of the Bethanys answers.

Teresa is paired with Fatima. "Sorry, I'm terrible at chess."

"And I don't know the game at all," Fatima says with a laugh. They play a low-stakes round as Teresa tries to explain the rules concisely. She also tries to let her opponent win but it doesn't happen. In the middle of their second game, the crowd is interrupted by a procession of self-driving wagons. The wagons taxi into the old hangar and loop in a half-moon to park at the center of the floor.

Some of the Bethanys clear the card tables away to make space; others move clumsily and less swanlike as they un-hitch the wagons, which have been carrying a bounty of tall, cumbersome boxes under canvas slipcovers. Bethany Two rips off the slipcovers one by one to reveal twenty-four automatons as tall as statues.

Each figure has a comically wide duck-shaped head with bulbous eyes like old Chuck E. Cheese animatron-ics. Teresa glances up at the duck in front of her. It has a hamburger bun–colored beak that flattens inward to the face, giving the impression of wry pursed lips. Covered in feather-like plush fur and dressed in a smock, the duck appears to be sitting at the edge of a giant cabinet with a chessboard painted on the top. Chess pieces are set up to play. The duck has human-shaped hands with five thin fingers in orange gloves. It taps a button on the side of the cabinet. There's a creaky rocking-chair-at-grandma's-house sound as its doors open slowly. She looks inside the cabinet. To the right, there's an empty space, and to the left are the automaton's guts: clockwork, gears, and pin-barrel machinery of the kind that could power an old-timey player piano. All this technology has been around for centuries. Teresa realizes, as she looks over the clock-work again, that the automaton has done this to reveal to her that there is no puppeteer.

The Bethanys pass out stools to the trainees and en-courage them to take a seat and play with these peculiar opponents. She remembers what the first Bethany she encountered told her—"there is nothing to win"—and assumes, with some confidence, that however she performs she still has a job at the end of the day. Still, the duck's snide face and the unpleasant creaky noises it makes inspires her to try to defeat it—which she does, twice.

After lunch, Teresa's group follows the Bethanys through another corridor. They arrive at a windowless office room with the twenty-four duck-head automatons scattered across the carpeted floor. The trainees laugh as they realize how the contraptions work: puppeted from the inside after all.

Bethany Three demonstrates with one of the ducks elevated on a podium. She taps a button on the side, the same button that the duck earlier—seemingly on its own—pressed to reveal itself. It opens, showing the clockwork and gears to the left and empty space to the right. She makes herself small and sits in the empty space and waves her arm to the other side of the cabinet behind the clockwork. Teresa can see it now. The gears and springs, which she had assumed extended from the back to the front, in fact cover another empty space.

"This is how you disappear," the Bethany says. "There's no magic trick to it. Just hide where they don't expect." The young woman crawls to the space behind the clockwork until it disguises her entire body.

Teresa taps the side button on the duck's cabinet before her. She notices how the clockwork is arranged to suggest depth, but the layer is hardly half an inch thick. She crouches to enter the empty space to the right. Feels cramped and a little cold in there, but safe; she crawls to the space behind the clockwork. It's not bad. Not unpleasant. Just weird to be doing this and for this job that she still doesn't understand. There is a touch screen at the top of the box with a digital image of the chessboard. It displays the chess moves in real time and registers actions as the person inside the box inputs them.

The Bethanys load the ducks onto a self-driving wagon. Teresa, still crammed in the cabinet, is surprised to feel ebullient rather than dogged with claustrophobia. She just spent all day learning a magic trick. The wagons enter Turing Hall and the whole class laughs with abandon. A rare moment of lightness. Now everyone is in on the joke.

"Strange town," Al says on the bus back, from his seat across the aisle from Teresa. Outside his window is the old stone commuter rail station with its clock tower under scaffolding. "This right here looks airlifted in from Stratford-upon-Avon."

"I grew up here," she says.

"Huh. What's it known for besides an ancient train station?"

"Shoe factories that closed before I was born. Sacco from Sacco and Vanzetti. Not much, I guess."

Usually the trainees ride the shuttle in silence back to South Station. But the drills with the ducks loosened everyone up. People on the shuttle are talking loudly, laughing and getting to know each other. Where are you headed back to? they ask one another. Abril takes the commuter rail and two buses back to her boys and her boyfriend in Quincy. Ricardo rides the subway to his house in West Roxbury, which he shares with his daughter and grandchildren. Nichelle goes to babysit her sister's kid in Mattapan, where she spends the night sometimes. Ordinarily she'd return to the apartment she shares with three roommates in Davis Square. Xavier unlocks his bike at the station and cycles home to Nubian to his parents' apartment, where he lives.

Maryvonne goes home to her studio in Braintree and her two fat calico cats. She will fall asleep watching sitcoms on her tablet device. But before that, on the bus, she bristles when Nichelle asks where the woman at the front desk takes her in the mornings. "I started training a couple weeks ahead is all," she says, looking down on her phone.

Al walks home to the North End. Teresa walks to the North End with him. She was just about to turn toward the Framingham commuter line platform, as always. But he was standing behind her and asked, "Do you want to get something to eat?"

7

Outside South Station, there's a narrow walkway of gardens that twists in parallel to the wharf. A new park; it's only been around for twenty years, converted from what had been a highway lane and named after one of the Kennedys. It looks like a tennis bracelet on a map. There's a merry-go-round in the middle with metallic paint and lights and classic horses that suggests it has been anchored here for at least half a century.

Teresa walks with Al along bushes of hydrangea. He lives in the North End. It's okay. His place belongs to his brother, a lawyer, who has a family and house in Framingham and isn't around to use it. She mentions quickly that she's living with her mother near Framingham because it seems like he won't judge her for it—he doesn't. To their right is the fancy hotel with a stone archway open to a view of the harbor and a cloudless sky. A teacher once told Teresa that Julia Child lived there when they passed it on the way to the Children's Museum on a field trip. She didn't know who that was at the time, she was only seven or eight. "A chef, a famous one, famous for Boston," the teacher said. Teresa had liked the idea that someone was famous for food and famous in this place and that they lived in a hotel instead of a house. It sounded like a good life for a grown-up.

Seagulls cry overhead as they pass the aquarium, where the last of the tourists shuffle out. There are kids carrying plush fish and foil balloons. Al Jin is so quiet at work, but here in the summer evening sunshine he springs to life. He's got a story about the time he got lost on an elementary school field trip to the aquarium. She wants to tell him about the Children's Museum, but maybe it's not very interesting to share. Either way he keeps talking. There are tall ships docked in the harbor and he knows what they are and all their names. The *County Castlebrook Earl* is his favorite, a real scrimshaw-worthy wonder of sails that made its way to the city from Nova Scotia just this month. Over there—that place with the umbrellas—has the best mussels. And over there, that path on the Harborwalk proper, is where he takes his bike on Sundays. He talks very fast, cut with quick mad laughter that happens even when the things he says are not so funny. He plans to volunteer at the recovery center over the holidays. Plans to fix his brother's telescope and chart the courses of Mercury and Mars in the journal that his brother gave him for his birthday. Plans to reserve a lot in the community garden next spring to grow blueberries, kale, and snow peas. Plans to move out of his brother's place in a few months maybe to Adams Village or Uphams Corner. Before then, he'll take his little nieces to the Ice Capades or whatever it's called nowadays.

"Have you been to the cranberry bog in Foxboro?" he asks. A tourist bus passes by as they approach the crosswalk at State Street. "Only the one in Plymouth," she says. "And not, like, regularly." It's not an easy bike ride, he says, but on a Sunday, when there aren't any commuters, the roads to get there aren't so bad. He rubs his head and looks around. She wonders if he feels the same way in crowds as she does: confused and overwhelmed, but not unhappy to be there.

"The place we're going is the best Italian food I've had and here you can't miss," Al says. They walk through his neighborhood with its cobblestone alleys, laundry hanging from lines, and old coffee shops cluttered with antiques. Under bright awnings with signs in bronze script, people dine outside the restaurants, drinking wine, eating pastas and dark green salads with slivers of Parmesan. And on the street corners are inexplicable dudes lingering about in packs of four or five. Each dressed in cargo shorts and athletic recovery sandals. She has only ever been to the North End a few times, usually on dates, and each time she has wondered if the towns in Italy are anything like this. There wouldn't be frat guys, Teresa thinks. Or maybe, with all the American tourists and students studying abroad, they are authentic to the place this part of town is meant to re-create. Maybe both cities changed together—for the worse, but still there's something nice, she thinks, about matching the authenticity of a place in a neighborhood created out of homesickness. She wants to tell him this, but something else comes to mind.

"That's Paul Revere's house," he says, pointing to a moss-colored monochrome wood house tucked between brick buildings that don't look quite as old. They turn on Moon Street and circle around a pastry shop.

All the names and places and ideas he's thrown at her all evening flutter between her ears as she tries to keep up with his conversation. It's nice, this attention. She has to drain out some anxiety in her head to make room for all the new fascinations this man has given her.

"Al. Do you know—" He seems like he would know. "How are the flowers in the lobby silver? Those flowers are fake, right?"

"They're real. Spray-tinted silver. I noticed a smudge on one of them. Planted vertical in stacks, I bet. The shelving probably looks like an egg crate when plants aren't in it."

"I don't like those flowers."

"I don't like them either."

A crowd of guys in cargo shorts blocks their way on

the sidewalk. To pass them, Al and Teresa cut through a garden with day lilies and small statues and a stone path to the open doors of a Catholic church, where more tour groups are wandering about. The place is historic, or at least very old. "We can go inside," Al says.

They sit in the pew in silence as a mix of tourists and the devoted speak in whispers and walk slowly. She looks over the painted crucifixes and up at the ceiling that ascends in a golden spiral to the fading sun. Gold light washes in and illuminates the pews. Heavy lanterns from the balcony cast a warm glow on the priests in navy tweed robes who walk by with soft footsteps. There are stained glass windows and murals of saints in bathing suit colors like yellow, teal, and coral. A small old woman with a shawl over her heavy shoulders drops coins in the donation box. She struggles with a match before she lights a candle and whispers something. There's a breeze from the open doors on the side to the doors open in the back. Teresa is overcome with emotion that catches in her throat. Everything before her feels so real and immediate, intense and stable, in this moment and place. She worries she might cry and embarrass herself. It's all good, Teresa's happy, but she feels recognized and seen in a way that hasn't happened in a while. Al's company feels like a loss of privacy, a disruption to the solitude she's been accustomed to; but also, it feels kinda nice.

It is dark now. The end of the main street is residential except for a corner restaurant that Al points to. It feels busier than it is because of the cramped space but it isn't loud and there are only a few diners. The restaurant sounds like string instruments on a tape deck and couples whispering to each other. The rooms are tightly decorated with embroidered curtains and patchy carpets. Little brass chandeliers, some with prisms missing, dangle from the ceiling. Everything seems to be a half size smaller than it should be. The tables are little. The lamps seem too small. All the tables with red-and-white-checked tablecloths are taken. They sit by the bar. Even the tarnished old silverware is oddly dainty.

"Three hundred years this restaurant has been around," he says. "I like that. They'll tell you about their grandparents' grandparents who worked here."

Teresa has her elbows on the bar and holds her head in one hand. "How is the neighborhood so resilient?"

"Resilient? It's not," Al says. "The family that runs this place commutes in from Holbeach. They probably know someone who knows someone who helps them out on the rent but that's not always enough. I've only lived here for a little while and I've already seen a couple places like this close down." He grabs a roll from the basket and rips it apart. "You might notice more places than usual around here are all cash. Not AllOver/AllCash. Like 'cash only,' as in, that's the way we do business here—got a problem with cold hard paper?"

The waiter, an old man, takes their drink orders. Al asks for sparkling water with lime and Teresa orders the same.

"If I wasn't tied to Boston—emotionally, I guess—I'd go to Las Vegas," he says. "I like Vegas. Everyone is a lowlife but they are transparent about their low-livelihood. Not like here, where people work to hide it."

"I've never been."

"It's close enough to LA, but not LA, so it gets all the losers and the chiselers who couldn't make it there. People who got run out of town owing a bunch of people money. That kind. The ones so unreliable that you know exactly where you stand with them. That's who lands in Vegas and I love them."

He orders a bunch of things for them to split and the food is served straightaway. They snack on giant olives and stuff their rolls with prosciutto and cheese.

"Not a lot of temptation for me there, actually. It is not my kind of risk," he says between bites. "I stayed in an area that felt Soviet, maybe? In a good way? It was a street full of high-rise hotels, fairly empty, dirty but not filthy, and real cheap, like thirty bucks a night. Thirty-five with a free breakfast buffet. There were marquee signs in the front with movable letters, and some art collective guerrilla art project went and rearranged them each day like refrigerator magnets. Every morning was a new sentence and different words were upside down for emphasis or the sentence was rearranged in a way that still made sense but looked confusing like 'Don't put all your baskets in one egg.' But more clever, you know."

Teresa pauses with recognition. "Sounds like the Parallax 3. Based in LA, but they get around. From that Barbara Kruger generation. A little didactic, slogans and stunts that must have sounded more subversive in the seventies, but they're interesting."

"You've seen them too?"

"I did some research on them." She remembers the months she spent making intra-library loan requests and scanning microfiche at the Brooklyn Library. "Only briefly. I was writing something for an old job I had. It was for a museum weblog."

"Well, I loved seeing it. And that city. I'm not sure how to put this but I like being somewhere that it's okay to amount to nothing."

"I need to get out that way. I don't gamble but I like the idea of the desert," she says.

"What I like is the line between the rich and the very poor feels unstable and circumstantial. Not like here, where everyone sizes you up immediately. I mean, I love my brother, but even my brother is like that. Something about Massachusetts does that, I think. It's not like that in New Hampshire or Rhode Island—at least not in the parts of Rhode Island that would have me. My brother hates Vegas." He's wolfing down his food and talking fast between bites. Too fast for her to say much of anything. She's trying to think of the farthest she's been out west and remembers a wedding in St. Louis she went to for a friend from college.

The bartender serves negronis to another couple at the bar. He's a young man. Maybe the waiter's grandson. She notices the words "La Famiglia" tattooed on his forearm in calligraphy-like script while he stirs the drinks.

"I lived in New York City for a little while," she says.

"I like New York when it feels like the smallest town in the world. Like you'll break up with someone and see them in the park the next day," he says. "Not that it's happened to me. But it always strikes me as funny that somehow people don't run into each other in Boston like that."

She doesn't want to ask, but she would like to know. "Before this, you were—?"

"A lawyer. Sort of."

"Like your brother?"

"He went to a better school. I reviewed documents. He helped me find work. It was okay but unsteady, and it's hard for me to work without structure . . ."

The tiny restaurant seems even smaller now. Teresa pulls her elbows close and crouches into the bar table instinctively, as though the place were caving in. Feels like they are sitting at a wood ruler from a school supplies kit.

"I could read and write when I was fucked up," he says.

Later Teresa will struggle to remember when it was in the conversation that he said that he only feels normal on heroin. She will hear it clearly in her head, in his voice, "The only time I feel normal is on heroin," but distrust that he was ever so declarative about a subject he approaches with such precise and insinuative language. This is the moment in the conversation that it seems most likely that he says those words, but he never said that. She will piece this sentence together into a memory, edited from rambling paragraphs, a flood of words he let loose that dance around this general idea. "I feel normal on heroin." Just the same, she will remember in the morning that he is divorced and forget how she learned this about him. There was a flood of words from him, and in it he gave the drops of an answer.

There is a pause. Not an awkward one.

"It's the time I don't remember that makes me grind my teeth real hard sometimes. When I went to sleep, I was thirty-seven. When I woke up, I was forty-six. I slept nine years. Nine years of nothing."

"You're forty-six?"

"Fifty-one now."

"You're fifty-one?"

"Yeah. How old are you?"

"Forty-eight. Can I ask—" She pauses. Maybe she doesn't want to know.

"Go on."

She tries to think of another question, but nothing else makes sense. "Why did you get into it so late?"

"I got into it early and went back in. I keep learning

the same lesson and that is, even if you are lucky enough to bounce back, most people don't want to deal with you again." He looks at his glass of sparkling water and blinks slowly. "It doesn't matter if you get back on your feet. They have their memories of who you used to be. And maybe you should let them hold on to that . . ."

It is cold in this tiny Italian restaurant that feels even smaller as he talks. The plates look like sand dollars and the cups and silverware like a dollhouse spread. She listens to the violins on cassette tape as he pauses before continuing. "Or else you will lose yourself in trying to convince people that things are different now. That you are different now."

Teresa relates to that statement. She can't understand why. And if she were to say so, as someone from a vastly different experience, it would be like the shallow "I know how it feels," which no one wants to hear at a funeral. Unsure of what to say, she looks at him and hopes her face telegraphs the lack of judgment that she genuinely feels.

"So things have been good for five years."

"More like two but good enough."

8

Al says thanks as the waiter refills his water glass. She notices how quiet they've been, whispering to each other like all the other couples in the restaurant. It is what he's saying that is loud. He was born in Trowbridge and moved to Florida in junior high. When his brother—younger brother—moved back north for school, he followed and cleaned up.

"It sounds like things are finally turning around for you." She is embarrassed at how trite those words sound and even worse that she should meet his honesty with dishonesty.

"Yeah. Different." She notices his hand in his lap is in a tight fist. He mumbles something about feeling underwhelmed professionally but being more aware of his surroundings now. He couldn't handle it, he says, when his world was measured out in swivel chairs, ironed shirts, and PDF files. He needed a barrier to shield himself from the sharp edges and transactional demands on his time. He can stay clean when he isn't pretending, when the people he deals with are real people.

When they walk out the door, it occurs to her that she has no idea who he actually is and all his talking over dinner might have made him more distant.

"It's late. I need to catch the commuter rail—"

Outside she has a sense of being close to the harbor even though she can't see it. The air is salty. The expanse of cloudy blue darkness farther down the street looks fit to jump in. She could cannonball dive from where they stand and disappear in the salty mist.

"You can stay with me," he says. "I can sleep on the couch. It's a nice place."

It is a nice place. Across the street and three floors up. There are no signs of Al in the apartment except his bike. All the furniture is tasteful and beige and ordered from the same four internet companies. The walls are red brick.

There is a box of Girl Scout cookies on the kitchen island with a note beside it: "Don't eat these at once!" From his brother. He'd come by earlier to pick up a few things. Al opens an empty drawer by the sink and puts the item from his pocket in it. They sit on a stiff couch upholstered in a heavy basket weave and drink filtered water with lemon.

He tells her about a friend of his that he is worried

about. Joshua cleaned up but he had to move back in with his father, somewhere in nowhere Minnesota. His father got him a job at Lowe's and they worked together at the same store until April, when his father died. He's going to lose the house and he misses his dad. "I call him sometimes and I tell him that he made his father proud. He got himself together, and his father got to see it. He's stuck in that town now, I guess." She imagines his friend and his father somewhere in the Midwest, driving to work together. Scanning items together in matching red vests. Maybe he used to pat his son on the back sometimes at work when no one was looking.

Al gets up and opens the box of cookies. "I don't know what other family Joshua has or what the shelter situation is like out there. I wish he could stay with me." He pauses and shakes his head. "We're lucky," he says, looking back at her.

"We are really lucky," she says.

"It's like a fitted sheet," he says. "Once you get one corner down, another corner rolls up. So sometimes, the thing to do is sit smack down in the middle of the bed and stretch your arms, maybe use your legs—make a snow angel—do what you can to keep all corners down."

She looks at him. "And for two years, the corners are . . . ?"

"Down. I might have to use a stapler. But down, for sure."

"I believe you." Teresa gets up and looks out the

window, wondering what kind of secret knowledge he has acquired and bottled up, the covert strategies, secret meetings, systems of measurements and techniques. Her mind flashes to a mental image of Al self-administering a tourniquet. She is horrified at her naivete and her restless imagination: How sheltered is she that her mind wanders in that direction? It doesn't make sense. She tries to focus on objects in his barren apartment—the bike, a purple Le Creuset on the stovetop—but her thoughts flutter and flash through the terrible images that show up on trashy news magazine programs. Hideous clichés. A burning spoon all rusty, a discarded syringe in a filthy hallway. Why does she have to be like this? She tries to shake this mental picture of him away and feels terrible. He is a good person who has only ever been good to her. She's the one with the problem. Maybe she should leave.

"What are you going to do with your first paycheck?" he asks.

What a thing to say. First paycheck? She laughs. It is so sweet. Like they are sixteen and working together at a pet store or as lifeguards on the beach.

"I haven't made any plans," she says.

Silence. He looks serious. Like he's about to say something important.

He points at her and smiles. "You should get a bike."

"A bike?" It would be nice, she thinks, if they had a car. He'd throw a set of keys over the kitchen island and she'd catch them. There would be a rental car, parked on his street. They'd pack it up with a big umbrella and beach towels and mount their bikes to the back. Drive to the Cape. Forget AllOver. Hop off the speed bumps and carousel around the rotaries. Find their way at perfect sky and endless water. Unwind in the sand with dogs tied to their beach chairs with an extended leash.

"All you need for a good life is a dog and a bike. I'm working on the dog."

His phone rings. He stands by the kitchen island, spins around, and faces the wall opposite her. "What do you want?" he says to the caller. He enters the bedroom and shuts the door, but she can hear him. "How come you didn't tell me earlier . . . I have a guest over . . . No, it's not like that . . ."

Back in the kitchen, Al explains. "My brother still uses the place like he did before I moved in. It's storage to him, most of the time, an investment property, but he sometimes sleeps here when he works late." He grabs another cookie and offers the box to her. She shakes her head.

"He's not coming now." He looks at his feet. "I need to get my own place. It's nice to not pay rent but it's not nice in other ways."

"My brother got messed up. He lost touch with us. I don't know where he is," Teresa says. She shakes her head again as if to refresh. "That was a while ago."

"Sometimes there's nothing you can do."

"If he's alive, he's got to be living like he's homeless,"

she says. The words cut into her throat when she says it. She's worried and wondered this thousands of times, but Al is the first person she's ever used that word with. His story about Joshua made her think about this. Teresa walks over to the kitchen island, where Al stands.

She remembers the last time she saw Mike. There was dirt over clumps of snow outside half melted. It was the fourth Wednesday in November, 2008 or 2009. She had come home from Cambridge and stayed in her child-hood bedroom that night. Mike had come around to the house, for the first time in months. Her father wouldn't let him inside. She watched from the window before tucking herself into bed, pulling the covers to her ears, but she could hear them. She could hear her father cry out in the cold on the front porch when her brother fi-nally left.

Outside the window, she sees lights in the apartments across the street and farther beyond. She wishes the apartment was theirs and they could furnish it. Put up a bookshelf; have some sense of their personalities ex-pressed in the belongings here. Teresa steps closer to the kitchen island and it brushes against her hips. She reaches for the box of cookies.

9

An unfamiliar alarm pierces the air and cuts out. Cabinet doors creak in another room above the patter of light footsteps on wood floors. She hears a coffee maker and a shower turn on as she pulls the covers down. Al's bedroom is as sparse and impersonal as the rest of the apartment. There's nothing in the room but a bed, a nightstand, and a cellphone charger cord extending from the outlet. The phone that would normally be attached to it is in the room past the door, which is closed.

Outside the window is a city alive. People are dressed for a run, dressed for work, walking with coffee and muffins in bakery bags, looking at their phones as they walk and listen to headphones. They walk their terriers and French bulldogs. This is the part of city life that she had taken for granted and hadn't realized she missed: the life-giving solitude and ease to the early hours. All these people are at the start of their clocks, each running on the promise of the first moments of a new day. She watches a dozen people pass at the cobblestone corner. Clean clothes, freshly washed faces, hair shiny in the morning sun. Birds are singing. She can see the harbor out behind the narrow buildings ahead—tranquil, rippling gray waters; just to look at it, with the boats and expanse of serenity, prepares a perfect morning for her. Everything seems to be blooming with a sense of purpose and possibility. The day has begun, which means this day might be a good one. At the corner, a runner crosses the street in neon mesh and clean white sneakers. She's not going very fast, but the runner is self-contained and driven as she makes her way down to the alley, like she's achieving a long-held goal. Teresa wishes she could run through the North End each morning like her. These are not graveyard shift workers; these are people for whom every morning is a fresh start. Rich people, probably, if they live in this neighborhood, but they all look like nice people.

She follows Al Jin to the Haymarket T stop, weaving through storekeepers sweeping the sidewalks before opening and restaurant workers already preparing for the lunch shift. A table-linens delivery van beeps as it attempts to park. The train arrives and she is overcome with the sense that where she is in this moment is perfectly right, that she is fully present and alive, just like she felt in church last night. She senses the energy and bewildering stimulation of the busy subway car full of commuters: all these people and their lives, each one is headed someplace, on the verge of what the day has in store for them. More intense is the feeling that she is a witness to his life. This is ordinary to you, she wants to tell him, but it is all new to me. It seems too intense to say this out loud. Would he even understand what she means? She could not gauge anything about him from his brother's untilled apartment, but the short commute seems like a clearing in the woods, another step forward. She grips the subway pole tightly and looks at her feet.

"Are you okay?" he asks.

"Yeah. Sometimes I get overwhelmed in crowds."

They ride the shuttle in a row together. Out the window, Render Falls is gleaming with another look of promise and possibility.

"Hey, kids, want to go for a ride?" Philip is waiting for them outside the building. "You, you, you, and you," he says, pointing at Teresa, Al, Nichelle, and Abril, the first trainees to step out of the shuttle.

There's a CR in the lot. A bright ripe blueberry of a vehicle glistening in the morning light. The vehicle is larger than she expected. About the size of a passenger van.

Nichelle circles around the front of the car, glancing

skeptically. "You mean it's not bullshit? We really can ride in this thing?"

"Sure can. She drove me to work. It was the finest fifteen minutes I've ever experienced in a vehicle. Your mileage may vary, of course, but I don't think it will."

Doors on either side switch up to the sky like a pocketknife and reveal a pristine off-white interior. Teresa and Al grab the two seats in the front facing back. Nichelle and Abril sit opposite. Teresa clicks on the recline button. It extends fully like a daybed, revealing how much space they have in the carriage unit. She adjusts the seat to a comfortable upright position.

Abril looks out through the open doorway latch. "Where will this take us?"

"Up North Howland Drive and back around the block," Philip says. "Enjoy!"

The doors switch back. There is no clunk to it. The closing doors sound like a feather swish. As the CR makes its way through the Render Falls lot to the exit, Nichelle opens a discreet glove compartment on the door with a wireless charging port inside. "I'd play some music but my phone's back at the front desk."

Teresa has been in a limousine once in her life: junior prom, her friend's father had had a good night at the Raynham dog track. She felt overwhelmed by the length of the vehicle and its amenities. The seats were quilted leather, possibly pleather, and a metal strip under the windows included a bank of a dozen push buttons that controlled the speakers. Another bank of buttons on the ceiling triggered different kinds of lights: pink lights, green lights, strobe lights, lights that beamed from the floor up to the ceiling, lights that twinkled.

The interior of the CR has no bells or whistles or pink lights twinkling from the floor, and it feels extravagant in its simplicity. Inside smells like wet flagstones and lemon. A silky-feeling seat belt hugs Teresa tight without pinching. The taupe seats, upholstered in leather smooth as a pebble, cushion and embrace her. The headrest and backrest support her shoulders; the winged seat curves to meet the backs of her knees. She remembers that the original Egg chair was designed for a Danish airline. When she first saw a photo of it, she had wondered how supportive the chair felt and whether its shape was only decorative. This seat feels like it was custom-made for her.

Overhead are luggage racks on either side, touch lights, and a closed compartment at the center of the ceiling. Abril pats at it. A dual-side screen opens up and projects AllOver animations as a default screen saver until Abril finds the remote and the screen folds back closed. The simple presentation to the interior makes the view all the more spectacular. Panoramic windows offer an unspoiled picture of outside in passing with the glare of the sun filtered through photochromic window tints.

When was the last time Teresa was excited to ride in a vehicle? That limousine was interesting, but when she thinks on it, nothing tops how she felt, in kindergarten, carpooling with a friend, riding in the back of the station wagon her friend's mother drove. That tiny bench of a seat in the trunk, where she and her friend would sit side by side, that was the best. In her seat in the CR, facing the rear, she's reminded of the view from the station wagon trunk: sitting in the back, feeling small, watching the world move farther from her as the car drives her away.

"I wondered if this might feel like floating on air but it feels normal," Nichelle says. "Just like a normal car drives. Well, like a normal electric car."

"They'd have to fix the potholes to make it smoother," Abril says as the CR dips at a crack as it turns onto the street. "AllOver would need to pay taxes to do that. But I'm going to assume our conversation is being recorded so that's all I'm going to say about that for the next half hour." She looks out on Pleasant Street. "Now this car, I'm really liking this. Very nice. But you can tell exactly who they expect the customers to be."

"Not us," Nichelle laughs.

"City strivers. The really rich will stick to Porsche and Bentleys," Abril says. "This just shouts to the road that any passengers inside are not from around here."

Their conversation is interrupted by a gust of wind flapping against the window and raindrops tapping. The pitter-patter of drops turns to heavy rain.

"Isn't this something," Nichelle says. "I thought these cars don't hold up in the rain. How is it turning around the block so smooth? No glitching out or anything."

Windshield wiper blades furiously swipe left and right, operating with the same autonomous precision as the rest of the CR. Teresa and Al swivel around to watch the window clear. "Strange," he says. "I wonder if the wipers are there for our benefit. So we can look out?" The other windows are speckled with rainwater but they all can see, through the windshield glass, familiar street-lights and the slippery parking lot at Render Falls fast approaching.

The CR enters one of the old hangars behind the building. Colored tape marks diagonal arrows and grid patterns on the floor. The vehicle moves along one of the taped paths toward the back wall, where there are tall gold machines lined up in rows like oversized chess pieces.

Each machine has a different end effector: pinchers and hooks of different sizes for different tasks. Some of the machines grip boxes on a conveyer belt in movements that are humanlike and tough as they move these items onto motorized shelving units. Robots with cranes at the ends of their arms stand motionless like resting boxers. Teresa watches as a machine with a screwdriver end effector attends to an empty CR on a four-post lift. All the gold machines have neon-colored wires circling around their bases to the floor like ecstatic maypoles in chartreuse, citrus orange, pink, and yellow, bright as highlighter pens. Farther in the back is the empty chassis of a CR stripped to its suspension and axles next to parts of a vehicle body disassembled beside it.

The CR doors switch up and Teresa feels assaulted by the noise. The robots are screaming: tut tut tut taaah tut zap zap zap wooshhh wooshhh; ungreased wheels, staccato drills, throbbing pulleys, rubber against metal, and other synthetic wails. The sound clobbers together and intensifies with the additional clamor of perforated metal. That sound is Philip and the rest of the group, stepping down with pounding footsteps from a scaffold stair tower to a raft-like white block in the center of the hangar floor.

It's intolerably muggy in the hangar, and with the clanging sounds and the smell of grease and heat, Teresa feels dizzy. She leans forward with her hands pressed into her knees.

A sharp noise cuts over the din with a chiseled sound like a knife against porcelain. Teresa looks back at the CR. The roof has split open.

Something appears to be hovering above the vehicle. It looks like a deep purple feather or an aubergine bird's nest. Teresa blinks. It's dark, and with all the multicolor wires and shiny machines, she finds it hard to focus.

The bird's nest begins to rise. It billows up a few centimeters.

There's a clang and a piece of white rubber pokes up at the exposed top of the roof. It looks like a finger, now five appear—it is a finger, a hand. A human hand grips the metal sides of the CR roof from inside like any driver clutches a steering wheel.

10

She Who Gives the Least F*cks clutches both sides of the open CR roof. At the height where she is positioned, she catches some of the flowing air from a single ceiling fan above. Her oversized white T-shirt billows out as she looks down on the group.

First she glances at the four passengers, standing just outside the CR. Teresa wants to look away, but she makes eye contact with Maryvonne and it stings. Light-headed, from the heat and noise, Teresa feels confused shame.

"I don't understand," Nichelle says, looking back at Philip. "What's Maryvonne doing up there?"

"Was she . . . driving this?" Abril says.

Teresa has a nagging sense that she should apologize to the woman, and for what she doesn't understand yet. It would be hopeless anyway; She Who Gives the Least

F*cks is too high up above her head, and she'd have to shout over the cries of the golden robots.

A massive robot with a crane end effector juts toward the CR. It finds a hook in the back of the harness Maryvonne is strapped in. There are murmurs from the crowd. "What the . . ." The machine lowers Maryvonne to the hangar floor with slow pendulum swings.

Teresa thinks about her ride with Al, Abril, and Nichelle: What did they get out of it? Thirty minutes around town: a distance someone could bike or even walk. It was unnecessary. Is this just another stunt by AllOver? It feels like a lesson, but for what? To show that everyone is profligate, everyone is capable of cruelty in places they're not looking? Too stunned by her guilt, Teresa remains silent as the trainees follow Philip back to Turing Hall.

"In the 1700s, Wolfgang von Kempelen blew everyone's mind in the Habsburg court with his invention, an automaton that could play chess," Philip lectures. "You experienced a replica of it yesterday. Our Mechanical Duck is not dissimilar to what entertained the likes of Benjamin Franklin and Napoleon: 'The Turk,' a regrettable name AllOver does not condone, but I must share with you this relevant history. Here's a fact that I find fascinating: Alexander Graham Bell invented the telephone because he believed the Turk was real. That is to say, he reverse engineered a magic trick. Belief in the Turk sparked a full century of bleeding-edge, tomorrow-building opportunity."

Philip looks at Teresa. "You believed in the CR, didn't you?"

She looks at the floor and says nothing.

"Soon enough, AllOver execution will match its dreams. Until then, a working prototype calls for real human intelligence. We can't waste time; this is far too important. Society has to adjust for driverless cars now or else progress will get strangled by red tape. With the CR on the road this year, municipal governments can pass legislation approving more bike lanes and pedestrian-only areas. That's once-in-a-lifetime progressive change, reclaiming city streets for the people and working toward a greener planet, all because it shows the writing is on the wall for the automobile in America. No more sprawl, no more pollution. If the telephone brought about a century of opportunity, what the automobile has offered society is much more complicated. One might say, instead of progress, this technology has been regressive. The CR is the natural solution to highway bloat and gas-guzzling."

Philip presses his clicker and a new slide appears on-screen showing a cross-section illustration of a CR. In addition to the battery and other parts in view, partitioned under the roof is a body. A human body. It looks distorted and awkward like pink clumps of wall insulation.

"So this is a stopgap, and I understand you may have concerns about job security. You have nothing to fear. AllOver has an internal program for all workers at risk of losing their jobs to automation. They might put you on the customer service team or another kind of role. You're part of the family now and AllOver will make sure that you stay close. And I saved the best for last: the rate is fifty an hour," Philip says with a grin. "That's twice what was quoted on the phone to each of you, and you have the 112 AllTogether-United employee-involvement shop to thank for that."

Teresa looks around the room as Philip calls a break. Now she can see the cohort for what they share. It seems obvious, from the moment she sees it, but it never occurred to her earlier. Every trainee in the hangar has dark hair. There's something else they all have in common: slim, compact bodies. It is a room of ectomorphs, each one of them about five and a half feet tall, give or take a couple inches. Long limbs and short torsos. Bodies small enough to hide.

Teresa continues to feel guilty for the CR test drive when she boards the shuttle to South Station with She Who Gives the Least F*cks. And she feels guilty for sizing up the woman on account of a dumb tote bag slogan. She can't even remember the woman's real name—Maryanne, Maryellen, Marybeth, Marilou, whatever it is, Teresa will remember it next time. Her ride earlier, and Philip's reveal, appear to her as both sides of the same coin. How sheltered Teresa was in that car, chauffeured through her dirty hometown; how could she have imagined this wasn't the task she signed up for—why would she think she's above it? She sensed it from the very first day that even the nice bagels and croissants and coffee were too good for her.

It is still light out on the bus from Framingham to Brixboro. In each town it passes, she notices houses with signs outside displaying the names of candidates for various selectman and school board posts. None of them are people she's heard of and nothing on the signs says what they believe.

At home, Teresa walks through the creaky front door. There's a note on the counter. Her mother wants her to take a stack of boxes out to the shed.

There's a key and a flashlight next to the note. She could wait until tomorrow, but if her mother wakes up first, she'll complain. Teresa grabs the boxes and walks outside where the crickets and katydids are chirping. She holds her flashlight steady as she pushes the rusty passkey into the lock to the shed. It gets stuck.

Teresa wiggles the key. The lock feels gummy. As she pulls the key back, the carcass of a bumblebee drags out with it. Half of it; the other half of its body is still mushed up in the lock.

"Shit," she cries out as she drops to her knees. Teresa takes the key and grinds it in the grass. She presses it deeper in the ground, rubbing it clean, exfoliating the metal in dirt before pointing her flashlight on it. The excess insect parts are gone and she turns the key back in the lock. Trembling and nauseous, she forces the key past the remaining gumminess. The key and the lock meet where the rest of the bumblebee body is trapped within. Once the shed opens, she runs in to put her mother's boxes inside, then locks it closed. She rubs the key in the grass again to bury the rest of the departed bee.

She was afraid of this house as a kid. It was a living example of how lack of care traded in disturbing inconveniences. The dust made her sneeze. Anything in the fridge was likely to be speckled with mold. Once, she found maggots under the sink in a half-opened cat food tin. Her great-aunt's cat had been dead for months.

Teresa opens her laptop. She has no new messages. Out of curiosity, she begins to search her email for receipts from past ride-hail travel on Uber and Lyft. She studies the maps and looks over the fares. The emails include names and pictures of each driver. She remembers none of them. December 14, 2015: Fifty-Second Street to Union Square for $21.58 with Kareem. There was a performance at MoMA and afterward she went to a birthday party for a friend she hasn't seen in years. March 29, 2018. Dinner with an old coworker out in Lowell. It was too late to take the commuter rail. She ordered a ride back to her sublet by the Forest Hills T for $38.03 with the driver Chhay.

There were more receipts. In the city and out of town. Together and alone. The time she sprained her ankle and ordered a car to take her five blocks to work. "I'm all alone," she says aloud, in words that stun her as soon as she says them; words that ricocheted in her mind and forced their way out in private. The crickets are too busy to hear her. Words uttered in a daze like an incantation. She said it automatically, inexplicably, and outside of her own inner monologue, which continues to stir over the calculations, the hard data that confirms her memories, and the drivers who were faceless up until she saw their selfies and headshots in these photographs that appeared in emails that she never bothered to look at until today. Maybe she never saw the drivers' faces when they shared a car. Maybe they never turned around. Why couldn't she remember at least one of them? They also need someone.

11

Teresa has been fired six times in her life.

The first time was at Cedars in 1997. "Let go" would be the way to explain it. "You know Mary," her boss had said, referring to another sales associate. "There was a mistake in processing and she never received her commissions. I could only keep one of you after the holiday season and I hope you will agree this is the right thing for me to do." Why he explained all this to Teresa over the phone made no sense. It sounded like labor violations. It probably was, but it was her first job, and she had her whole future ahead of her.

The second time, it was Teresa's fault. She had failed to properly lock up the VFW bar, where she had worked as a barback in the summer between freshman and sophomore year in college. Stupidly. She thought the bartender was still inside and he would get to it.

That fall, Teresa took a job in medical transcription.

She would drive, after class, to an asthma and allergy physicians practice in Bridgewater to pick up a brown bag full of microcassette tapes left for her in the mail room. She got paid by the tape. The doctors were identical twin brothers, Brett and Andrew, but it was months until Teresa felt comfortable calling either of them anything other than Dr. Lewis. They were quarterback-handsome men in their midthirties with wavy brown hair. Andrew—the older brother by seven minutes—was the responsible one, while Brett played pranks on the office workers and drove a red Sebring convertible. She rarely saw Andrew, but Brett would pop his head out from his office to say hi and give her that kind of look to show that he noticed she was thin and very young.

Teresa liked pressing pause on the tapes using a foot pedal under her desk. It felt like driving. She learned so much that year about the reactions people have to ragweed and shellfish. She could type fast, but after three months, her fingers began to tingle. Then her wrists went numb. It hurt to pick up a pen, schoolwork became difficult, and she could only type in fifteen-minute intervals broken up with hour-long breaks. She didn't want to tell the office that she was having this problem because she figured they'd send her off with fewer tapes next time. It had to have been an arbitrary deadline, she assumed, continuing at the pace that was to the best of her abilities. If they really needed the tapes on time, they would call her, right?

When she returned to Lewis & Lewis Asthma and Allergy Physicians with a folder of typewritten notes, perfectly formatted, a week after the deadline, the office manager told her that there would be no more tapes for her in the mail room. Brett didn't poke his head out. That was the third time.

The fourth time was a slow fade-out. Her junior year at Amesfield State, she waitressed at the fancy place in town where professors met at the bar and students brought their parents. It had been an ironworks; really old, an early-eighteenth-century establishment, cozy with electric fireplaces, stone gables, and stained glass. Her first day, Teresa asked another waitress about those windows. The girl hugged her tray to her chest and said the stained glass was brand-new, to fit the theme of the place. Teresa was good enough at the waitressing basics; she remembered orders perfectly and could balance drinks on a tray without difficulty, but it's not like she's ever had the world's most bubbly personality. She could tell that customers thought she was cold, that she had an attitude. When it comes to smiling and eye contact, there's only so much that a person can fake. The more she tried to charm customers, the more Teresa felt drained at the end of her shifts. One day, when she looked at the week's schedule, she saw fewer shifts than she ordinarily worked. On the schedule after that, she had half as many shifts. The following week, her name wasn't on the schedule at all. The old ironworks is now the Iron Works, a coworking space or a start-up incubator. Teresa doesn't know how she knows this; perhaps she saw an ad for it on Facebook.

Jobs went, but they also came easy at that age. This is something she often thinks about at the Brixboro Y, when she goes swimming. And of course, that's not the full picture. In high school, often, she'd wander into a store like Waldenbooks and ask for an application like her father told her was a normal thing to do. She would look down when she asked for applications. It is always awkward to be face-to-face with people who have what you want. Then she'd write her name and address and phone number on the paper printout. Waldenbooks never called and she never followed up.

Cedars was easy because there had been a giant HIR-ING SEASONAL EMPLOYEES sign that she passed on her way to school. She entered the store and lined up near the hardware section. They conducted interviews on a card table and hired people on the spot. Come to think of it, everywhere she worked in those years, apart from what temp agencies arranged, happened because she entered an establishment with a NOW HIRING sign in the window.

After college, the process got easier. She could go to the career fair that her school hosted in the spring. It was held in the student union building, where there were booths for companies in the area like GE, Liberty Mutual, and Raytheon and nearly every university within fifty miles except for Harvard and Brown. She just had to walk in, talk to people briefly, and write down her contact information to be considered. It was there she found a good enough job: bank teller at a credit union.

The best part was counting what was in the vault; she felt powerful holding over a third of her salary in her hands, the cash wound in a $10,000 strap. She loved that the bank trusted her to do this. The worst was when customers got impatient when she counted bills twice. The other best part was handing little kids lollipops when they got their passbook accounts stamped or candy canes over the holidays.

All in all, it was a pretty good job. And fascinating, often, to match a face to a bank account balance. One time she had a customer with $236,013.83 in his checking account. He had his own business and floated money for vendors, but it shocked her just the same to see it. So much money and in an account for nothing, collecting paltry sums of interest, no more than a roll of dimes.

The only thing missing from the job was room to advance. Teresa didn't want to be a loan officer or to supervise the teller line. She returned to the career fair in the spring carrying copies of her updated résumé with a new bullet point under "WORK EXPERIENCE."

"Got to be meticulous for a job like that, right? Huh," said a representative from MassTech. Another great job. Lap twenty-five, she remembers this. She moved to an apartment off the Red Line in North Quincy and rode the T to Kendall Square every day. If she had stayed at MassTech, Teresa would have been rewarded with a fat pension soon, and she never would have been fired again.

But there was the fifth time. It happened her seventh year at the Brooklyn Modern, what the institution called department restructuring. An email caught her by surprise before breakfast, and she entered the conference room hungry. Jord, her boss, was there with a representative from HR. Teresa signed papers she was too startled to read properly and all she remembers of it now is thinking that, from that moment on, she would look back on this period of her life as though someone else had been living it. And she has.

The sixth time she was fired happened in lockdown, three weeks into the pandemic. She was newly hired as a data admin for a health insurer headquartered in the city; a last-in, first-out situation.

She had expected a year on rattling Green Line trains back and forth from Brookline to Park Street and a short, windy walk to and from Downtown Crossing. Instead she holed up in her bedroom, scrolling for advice in a private Facebook group for people in Massachusetts collecting unemployment benefits.

When she first logged in, she wondered if her friends on Facebook could see what she was doing. It was a secret group, but this was Facebook; she didn't trust that the social network hadn't broadcast her misfortune on everyone's public timelines between their photos of teenage children and home repairs in progress. Whatever apprehensions she had were less than her fears, sparked by confusing letters in the mail. Overpayment notices, voided overpayment notices. Sometimes an unfamiliar name with a mass.gov email address would request she provide a list of jobs she had applied to since April immediately. And in this Facebook group people crowdsourced the best way to respond to them.

Some of the users left comments, angry comments, thinking the Facebook group was the actual unemployment office and that they were not sufficiently helping them. "You just going to tell me that your supervisor will call me?" Others announced broader despair to a forgiving public.

> *I'm so sick of living in anxiety and depression because of all this. Every single day I wonder if I'm going to be told I owe 10k back in unemployment. Every day I feel like I'm doing something wrong or I'll accidentally become a felon because I don't understand the rules and our government and MAES is so friggin incompetent.*

The group was moderated by a blond woman who often illustrated her posts with low-res Minion memes or animated gifs of Minnie Mouse rolling her eyes.

For the 800th time! I try to keep this space welcoming and that means putting a stop to anyone who is here to make trouble. If your comment is along the lines of "there are plenty of jobs out there. Find a new job" I won't just delete it. I will block you. There are MANY reasons that people cannot return to work so mind your own freaking business. Thank you.

At nine thirty every other night, Teresa would click on the YMCA website and reserve a lane twenty-four hours in advance. Sometimes her web browser would stall and in a moment, all lanes would be booked up. She could walk to the YMCA from her apartment and leave behind the sound of her neighbors watching television loud and the stomping in the apartment above or her roommates in the kitchen always chattering on their phones and screaming about the dishes that had piled up. The Green Line trains would screech beside cars honking at every intersection. She'd navigate around the flurry of customers in and out of Whole Foods. In the rain, the people would jostle with their umbrellas and all the street sounds seemed louder. She'd scan her YMCA keychain pass and walk down the steps. The pool was in the basement. The volume of music in the aerobics class and the hum of treadmills would go down with every step until she entered the glass doors and heard nothing but the sounds of bodies slapping the water and the corners of the brightly lit basement trading a sough of echoes. It was a dreamlike respite from the noisy world, from the chemical taste of the cold air inside to the first dip in the shallow end. On her back, she could get lost in the patterns of rafters and piping above. The area was clean like her apartment was not. It was quiet in there, unlike the rest of the city. It made sense to her like the rest of the world did not. There was one rule she could follow, easy: stay in her lane.

Teal water, red and white lane dividers, black and white bunting from the rafters end to end. Human beings in wet spandex, ears plugged, eyes underneath mirrored goggles, bumbling in and out of the water, at a distance from one another, like astronauts, tiptoeing around the perimeter, out of place and out of time, unable to converse with one another, wholly focused on whichever point in this orderly space they were and intended to be.

She enjoyed the uncomplicated rituals to prepare for her swim, like lancing a new pair of goggles at the nose bridge for a perfect fit and covering her face with a light layer of olive oil so the chlorine wouldn't burn it red. She'd make soup, when she returned home, and read the Facebook messages that accumulated when she was out.

> *If u end up having to move all the time,over & again
> (nowhere to go bc mistakes happen even if it is not
> specifically about u or ur fault) (aka; homeless)living in
> Mass out of your car is not an option.not with winter
> coming.PObox is not accepted by Gov agencies who won't
> send correspondence to your yahoomail and if u don't get
> the correspondence,they claim to have posted u risk losing
> it all . . . (missing a lot apparently). living in the cheapest
> motels at 1500 a month(very expensive; rn esp) about
> to run out. Shelter is known as a business,so Gotv
> won't accept that,PostOffice says they can't use as a
> residence,relatives are not an option here. Can
> anyone help me,? Just wondering.*

Sometimes these strangers would find someone with something resembling an answer. "Online mailing address," someone commented on the post from the individual without a home. "There are addresses you can safely send mail to that are not PO Box. I just went through this because the postman is not trustworthy in the town where I live and you are right, MAES won't accept PO BOX."

Emails continued to arrive. "You have a new message from Mass Employment Security." She'd log into her account and find nothing. More threats, like one that stated her claim had been invalid, and she had to return the funds in total. There was a phone number on the letter. She'd wait hours on hold before sorting things out with the representative. It all felt like a job. It felt like a bad job.

But in the water, she regained a sense of purpose, she could forget all of this and everyone. Arms slapping the water, feeling small and powerful and machinelike, she was strong and fast, unbeatable in this race of only one.

12

BE NICE.

The words appear in bright green block letters on a slide. "That's rule number one," Philip tells the group in Turing Hall. "Passengers might not see you smiling in the nest, but you better believe they will feel the difference."

Rule #2:

NEVER RETURN TO A PASSENGER'S HOUSE.

"After a drop-off, forget the place, forget the passengers. You were never there," Philip explains as he paces back and forth on the podium. "It's in-state ride-share passenger protection law. Whether or not it applies to driverless vehicles, well, at this moment we don't want to go about challenging it." He looks out at the crowd. "Got it? Good."

Rule #3:

SAFETY FIRST, SECOND, ALWAYS.

"Everyone in this room is incredibly limber with phenomenal reflexes and hand-eye coordination. If I was coaching you as a lacrosse team, we'd crush it in the championship. In the CR, you put your physicality to a higher purpose. Protect the passengers and you protect your own butt too."

The room is noticeably less full than it was the day before. Teresa had thought about dropping out too. Falling into bed the night before, she imagined sleeping through her alarm. On purpose. No one would have witnessed this calculated mistake, but she feels compelled to attempt to tip fate whenever wracked with indecision. Possibly, she could find work that is better than this, but probably, Teresa thinks, if that were true, it would have happened already. Anyway, she had been too nervous to get any sleep. So here she is, tired and ready to contort herself like a pretzel to drive a self-driving car.

"I understand you might have concerns about safety." The crowd, what's left of them, look up at Philip. "These are fair concerns, but look, this is no Wright-brothers-at-Kitty-Hawk suicide mission. What you'll be doing is akin to what ship captains or truck drivers tackle every day. The biggest problem, you'll find, is a little tennis elbow here, some gastrocnemius strain, plantar fasciitis. And again, that goes with the territory. Airline pilots suffer more from repetitive strain injury than any other occupation. My advice is get a good massage therapist on speed dial."

Nichelle raises her hand. "How could anyone drive from LA to San Francisco in this position? That could take all day."

Philip explains that AllOver acquired defunct travel plazas on the West Coast and fixed them up as loading stations with shops from vendor partners like MeUndies and Blue Bottle Coffee. It's called the "intermission." Passengers grab food and move their feet while CR drivers—the "seers," he calls them—swap out. Smaller properties have been installed around cities including Boston. These pop-up garages are where drivers charge up or wait between rides and clean the carriage for the next passengers.

Teresa thought she misheard Philip before, like he could have been saying "steerers," but indeed he's calling the trainees "seers."

"Seers, really?" Abril says. "Well that sounds bleak. Cut to the chase. What happens in an accident? In what scenario do we live through a car crash?"

"The vehicle is built to the utmost standards—"

"What every carmaker says. I just want to know, who is going to ensure my body doesn't get pressed to a pancake in a junkyard car crusher?"

"It's collision-proof. We're talking NASA-grade physical security. Everything has been tested nine hundred times and yet again. In the case of drowning or atypical altercations there is an emergency pod exit that we will go over in a later session."

"We're just a small group of people," Nichelle says. "How is that going to cover demand for the cars?"

"For Rose Quartz, this is a sufficient fleet. If anything, we're over-hiring," he says matter-of-factly. "You'll wait around a lot. Could go a whole shift without a single passenger."

They pause for another exquisite lunch buffet—avocado slices, peach and burrata caprese, crusty breads—and regroup in the hangar-garage.

Looking past the gold robots and CRs lined up like a branch of oversized blueberries, Teresa notices something else moving. Silent, but quick on their feet, there are people moving around on the floor, the real human mechanics. From the stairs, the trainees can see the tops of the turquoise hardhats the mechanics wear but not their faces. It would be easy to mistake these workers for other machinery.

A mechanic steps toward a bare space on the cluttered floor. Teresa recognizes him. They went to high school together, she thinks. He was always pretty nice but she didn't know him well and doesn't know his name. Maybe he's a Facebook friend.

A CR starts and drives to where the mechanic stands. It poses before a gold robot with a hooked end effector.

Another mechanic, holding a mannequin in his arms, joins her old classmate in the middle of the garage. With its long blond wig and smooth protrusion of a bust, the unclothed mannequin appears to have been built to display juniors fashion. The mechanics arrange the fake woman to pose at an orange line marked a few feet from a robot arm. They steady the mannequin again and sprint to the other end of the hangar.

The robot arm makes a turbine-powered vibrating noise and beeps as its crane is lowered. Swaying back and forth, the hook finds the mannequin's belt. Fastening itself, the robot lifts the mannequin up and deposits the object in a hideaway on the roof of the CR.

Teresa tries to picture She Who Gives the Least F*cks being carried into the vehicle this way, but it doesn't seem possible. This seems like an overly involved process that could be just as efficiently completed with a ladder and step stool.

Now the driver's unit on the roof of the CR is open and visible to the group of trainees. Inside it, the mannequin rests over black arching cushions. Its arms dive forward and its plastic legs curl into the footwell with the gas pedal and brake posted to the back. The driver will need to kick back, heel before toe, to step on it. Both sides of the unit are blanketed with Mylar, like the reflective sunshade Teresa leaves on her mother's Impreza dashboard. Textured chain mail–like metal mesh drapes like spiderweb over the driver's head. Buttons and knobs and video windows wrap over the front panel like a cockpit.

There's a shrill alarm and red lights flash. The crane moves forward again and hooks the mannequin's belt to lift it out. Gliding back, the machine sets the mannequin on the floor. It tips forward and slams facedown on the hangar floor as the crane unhooks itself. One of the mechanics rushes over to take the mannequin back to the far corner of the garage. He drags it by its plastic handless right arm.

"Teresa," Philip says. "Go over to where the test model was standing and wait. The orange line. One of the floor guys will get you set up."

She moves, dazed and cautious, in baby steps to the edge of the platform at the end of their stairwell. It feels hallucinatory, in a familiar way that reminds her of the moments when she approaches the edges of a swimming pool. She hears a rhythm to the robot screams and clangor and looks for patterns in the candy-colored wire and tape crisscrossing the floor. She is plunging in.

A man in a turquoise hat is waiting. He takes her hand, his palm calloused and caked with grease, and helps her down the narrow steps to the floor, slick and sticky like a roller rink. Together they walk toward another mechanic in the middle lane. He holds a corset-size garment. It is more of a harness than a belt. He wraps it around her middle and she pulls her arms through two loops. It cinches at the back where a heavy brass ring pokes out. She looks up at the man's kind face. Rob is his name, she remembers now. He seems to recognize her too, but this is no occasion to talk.

Rob disappears with the other mechanic. Teresa stands alone in the center of the frenzy. She squints and the colors in the hangar blur as crepe paper streamers and ribbon candy. The tips of her fingers tingle; she feels light-headed and sore in the throat.

The robot arm startles her. Teresa screams. There's a dull stab at the small of her back where the ring stands taut. The machine foists her up like rice between the tines of a fork. Before she can register her discomfort, she's in the air, kicking the absence under her feet, waving her arms in circles from the shoulder like she could assert herself and fly to the top of the CR by herself. She tries to enjoy this moment of weightless surrender, but she sways involuntarily at a height that feels unsafe. The robot arm juts forward and lowers her into the car very slowly.

Her heart is beating faster. She can feel it now that she's snug with her belly curled over the cushions in the unit, latched like a pin in a deadlock. "That's the nest," she hears Philip explain to the others. The robot arm unhooks from the ring in her belt and thrusts back to its resting stance. Teresa's teeth clench. Her legs and arms shake as she assesses the CR interior. She can't see it, but she can feel the chain mail at the back of her head. Her hair tangles in its mesh holes. She leans her hips back; her forehead is pressed up to a rubber block to rest upon as her arms enter the straps on either side. Kicking back, her heels reach the rubbery pedals.

She takes a close look at the cockpit panel. Two screens show the view through the windshield and back window. Another screen shows live footage of the empty CR carriage. To the left and right are what would be side mirrors, if she were driving an ordinary car. There are buttons all over the right side. Beside each button is a Post-it note flag with quick handwritten descriptions of their functions. Next to the green button, it says "Passenger Audio." The note beside the purple button says, "Audio Connex," and by the yellow button, twice as big as the others, is a normal size Post-it note, on which "Emergency Only" has been scribbled. It confuses her, how her head faces back, while the car, once it moves, will go forward the opposite way. Through this mirror view upside-down, all she can see are wires and robots. Ahead is the closed garage door. She is uncomfortable, still, and clings to her discomfort. She knows that the moment driving the CR feels natural to her will be the moment she loses control.

She would like to be bad at this. She would like to be

so terrible at driving that she will have no choice but to quit. After processing the world outside from this peculiar angle, she pauses on the window to the interior. She knows how comfortable those pebble-smooth leather seats really are, much more comfortable than in here. There's a shrill cutting sound when the CR roof splits apart. The crane scoops her out.

Softly, as the machine lowers her, toe first, then heel, she touches the ground. For a moment, she feels as though she performed a great athletic feat worthy of a stadium. "Look at that. Perfect form," Philip says. He pats her on the back when she returns to the group. "It is easy. Like learning to ride a bike. Your body will adapt and snap into position before you can think about it."

Teresa's body did not snap naturally; or it did. She isn't sure.

"No, but really. What if there's an accident?" Nichelle asks. "How do we get out of there?"

Philip explains that in water or fire or any kind of accident, the top will open up and eject the driver's nest. Fully padded with a parachute, it is modeled after the exit capsules in a spacecraft and tests as ten times safer than any other kind of vehicle. Workers will be escorted immediately to the nearest AllOver headquarters for medical attention.

Now it's time to drive. The hangar doors slide open and the morning sun washes over the walls in brightness. Back inside the nest, Teresa loops the straps over her wrists and leans against the arch to look to the right of the screens. The hardest thing about it so far is the balance and sense of stress at her chest. Her eyes focus on a bright red button. "Autopilot," the Post-it reads. It works for self-parking and could briefly assist with automated steering.

Hesitantly, Teresa presses on the gas. Ten miles an hour increases to twenty as she drives from the hangar to the parking lot. Soon four other CRs join her: Nichelle, Fatima, Xavier, and Ricardo, all disguised. Philip instructs the group to loop around Render Falls. The seers double their speed as they run these laps and double again.

An outside observer would see four bubble-like electric blue cars, driving at about forty miles an hour around the old airport grounds. They would see nothing but driverless cars.

13

R ender Falls is an airport again for the first time in thirty years as a plane touches down to the parking lot that had been a runway before the twenty-first century. Philip shouts as he runs toward the Gulfstream glimmering in the sun. "Verma!"

There she is, gracile, regal, dressed in a white jumpsuit and chic cob-heel boots. That unmistakable starlet poise, from the top of the air stairs, glancing around at the antiseptic landscape: Vermont Qualline, in the flesh. She's flanked by two lean guys in sunglasses and expensive denim.

Vermont has flown in from Jackson Hole after delivering a keynote address on user privacy and data protection issues at the Ideas for Progress Festival. Philip stammers before her. "I've heard nothing but good things about your talk yesterday. Very wise of you to highlight these concerns with regard to users in the Global South."

Teresa can hear them from the CR nest. She presses back on the gas pedal with her right foot to receive passengers. The doors open and Vermont climbs in the car with a sense of familiarity that Teresa finds off-putting. Philip and the two dapper guys follow her in.

"Best ride I had was in Norcross in April," Vermont says, as she crosses her legs and settles in. "Got me all the way to Augusta without a break. I always ironically attend the Masters. I'm grateful that our CRs know how to step on it, when we need it; otherwise I might have made an entrance unfashionably late."

Blue Jeans looks at the sides of one of the hangars and scowls. "That's not the right polycarbonate for the job. I'll call the supplier to fix this." Black Jeans finds the charging station. Electronic music begins to play. "Lately I love the Inverted Telegraph in Primrose Hill," he says with a faint English accent.

"Love that one," Vermont says, nodding.

"An absolute must is Ghislaine Darby's in Mayfair. These cats remodeled an old council flat. All the furniture dates to the seventies and they serve variations on retro dishes, some stroganoff, lemon meringue cake, prawn cocktail, ham crepe. Serious creative spins on baked beans with mash. Then there's Cheque Puzzle in Islington by the canals. Manon Penthièvre's latest joint."

"Already been. Those tiny cakes with the salmon roe are quite nice, and the room with candlelights is the very best. But you know I hate to spend more than an hour outside my hotel whenever I'm in Londontown. It's the fog. It really gets to me." Vermont reviews an email she has just typed with her thumbs on her phone and presses send. "Pea-soupers! That's what you call them. Isn't that right? I always feel so . . . sooty when I step outside. I like Shoreditch in theory, but I need to breathe. Next time I'll stay in the countryside."

Teresa checks the screen with a view looking down on the four of them. They look well at home and cozy in the primordial leather seats. The arrangement strikes Teresa as funny. She first encountered this woman in this town, as a poster image, but Vermont would have no attachment to this place. Her poster had to be hanging in hundreds of Cedars locations, not to mention the magazine covers; all the Barnes & Noble and Borders racks where you could see her smiling out to strangers one-way. That's what fame is all about—claim to territory, without setting foot in it; your name and face travel beyond constraints of time and space.

Vermont looks out the window with a wary eye. "The seagulls around here. They're like rats. Filthy."

"Once you get to Kinshasa, Verms, you'll love this," Blue Jeans says. "Chez Poétique. Phenomenal cuisine and still off the beaten path even by the humble standards of the Dee-ROC."

Teresa smacks the passenger audio off. A window lights up on the inverted dash. It shows a map of the town with a red trail, snaking around the left corner before it circles back to the starting point. She presses on the automated ride button. And then she waits. The car steers on its own. It turns at the light. She doesn't have to do anything. It is only when the car comes to a shadowy point on the freeway outside Render Falls that a voice pipes though the intercom instructing her to drive a hundred feet and turn left. She continues at the automated voice's commands until she cloverleafs around and turns on the minor highway that gradually descends into downtown Stoughton.

At the corner of the street is a tree with windy lithe branches and small mauve flowers. The house has mauve shingles that are chipped but as bright as the flora. Teresa imagines a couple—her parents' generation, but back when they were young—deciding together they would paint their house to match the tree when it flowers. Maybe they took a flower to the paint store. Maybe she saw them in the paint aisle at Cedars looking for a perfect match among the card gradients. Sometime at this date in mid-September, but thirty years back exactly, they would have gone to Cedars together to get that paint. It makes her sad to imagine where this couple she has invented in her mind might be right now.

Down the road she notices some familiar sights. That army navy store. An old store selling window and awning decor, a barbershop, and the Portuguese National Club where her uncle used to bartend and her grandparents had been members.

She turns on the volume to the carriage as they pass the train station.

"Such strange architecture," Vermont comments, brushing her fingers through her hair. Vermont wears heavy rings on every other finger. "This train station. It's made of stone like a storybook castle but it's dingy."

"Very old and dingy, yes," Black Jeans says, as Blue Jeans also nods in agreement with her.

"And that clock tower is really old. Whole thing was built in 1888," Philip says. He had been silent for most of the ride.

"Probably the last time they cleaned it too," Vermont says. Philip slaps his knee. All the guys laugh with her.

Teresa turns off the carriage sound again and enters the Render Falls lot with feelings of relief. She sees, in the monitor to the carriage, that Philip has said something excitedly. Vermont squints with displeasure. Then she smiles and waves as the other three step out. Vermont stays inside. She pulls out her phone and makes a call.

Teresa assumes it will only be a short call. But the woman kicks up her feet on the seat where Black Jeans had been sitting. Twenty minutes pass, and for each of those minutes Teresa wonders if she has the wherewithal to quit. Where would she go—nowhere; only to be cursed to dwell in that living room slash bedroom in

Brixboro another seven months that, before she knows it, would drag on another several years.

Teresa wonders if the people in the carriage had any idea about the secret person riding in the CR, the one responsible for the ride. Philip knows, of course. But did he know the driver is her—did he care? And Vermont. Does she know someone is in the car, stationed above like an inmate escaping through ceiling ducts and crawl spaces, like a cockroach hiding in the kitchen walls? Vermont is vice president at AllOver, second-in-command of automotive or whatever the department actually is. How could she not know? Teresa yells into the space blankets and mesh, "Let me out!" It makes her feel worse. Vermont puts her phone in a platinum purse that matches her hair. Finally, Vermont exits the CR.

The billboard in Brixboro that used to say WE WILL BUY YOUR UGLY HOUSE has been replaced with a picture of Plum Sasha lounging in a CR. Her teeth and blue eyes are clear and perfect. She looks carefree and young. There's a retro eighties feel to the bubbly blue letters that read LUXURY. PRIVACY. SPOTLESS. PRICELESS. THE CR HAS ARRIVED. SEE IT!

Seer. It's a good name, Teresa thinks. It reminds her of Cedars. But what are they doing advertising in this crummy town some fifteen miles from the nearest Whole Foods? Looking for drivers, Teresa supposes.

There's another ad on TV with Plum, same clothes and same sneer, on the screen. She is in a car with a bunch of young people who are dancing in their seats to a hip-hop track that Teresa can't place.

"Try the new CR driverless experience," a hollow-toned woman says in voice-over. "Private and clean, unmatched comfort and ease. The possibilities are endless. This future is yours alone to try."

Teresa lingers on the phrase "driverless experience." It is no lie. The car is driverless. She isn't driving, exactly. She's part of the car. A seer is a car part, a battery. Like a bellhop-less elevator—that is, if an attendant had been stationed all the time, above the carriage, hoisting it up and down with pulley and rope, in lonely silence as people inside wait to arrive at their floor. How many elevators has she ever stepped in? At least once a week now for something or another. Twice a day, five times a week in the years when she worked in offices. And she never wondered or questioned how an elevator worked. That was the genius of the CR. Soon enough, people won't wonder how it works, and should they learn, they won't care. She's the ugly, fleshy part of a mollusk. It is the pretty shell that riders want; they want to be the pearl inside, contained in superior technology, with a perfect panoramic view of the world outside.

"That's where I work," Teresa says to her mother, sitting beside her on the daybed. "My job at AllOver is confusing to explain, but I like it. Hope you're proud of me." Her mother looks up and nods quietly. "Remember when Dad said he thought it could be a good company? It's that place in Stoughton. That old airport past downtown. I even met Honey Q's daughter at work. The country singer, remember him? His daughter is famous too."

"Oh?" Her mother looks back at the television.

"Prettier in person."

Her mother finishes the last of her biscuit, throws the paper plates and plastic fork in the trash bin, and returns to her bedroom. Teresa stays in the living room and watches more television. The living room is a bedroom again, where she sleeps in fits and starts.

A family of deer gallop past the window, illuminated only faintly by the streetlights. Two fawns nibble at the hosta leaves by the curb while the mother deer appears to keep watch. Teresa approaches the window to watch them as they prance across the road toward the yard of a neighboring house.

"Bye, friends," she says, whispering at the window like the window and the animals can hear her or understand. The lawn needs mowing. Teresa should take care of that. In the distance, over the sound of crickets, some kind of fox or fisher-cat is screaming like a kid with a skinned knee. A giant moth lands on the screen, desperate to enter the house and to luxuriate under the nightlight in the kitchen. She takes comfort, sometimes, in these moonlit transitions, when the suburbs and small towns turn wild at night—how swiftly nature takes over when the humans wind down. Teresa turns out the lights and lets the wilderness envelop their home.

She thinks back on the commercial. The illusion is so seamless, she never stopped to contemplate who was driving the CR on the screen. Who was ferrying Plum Sasha and her friends? She, of all people, should remember the human labor that is part of the CR deal. Did the seer receive extra money for appearing in the commercial? Or was it all a simulation over a green screen?

Maybe all this time she's been in elevators, there has been someone hidden above, lifting her up and letting her go back down.

14

I t's not a bad job. Odd, yes, of course, and sometimes painful. She experiences an oscillating throb from her knuckles to her knees. But less than ideal is not the same as bad. She has privacy, after all, no one can bother her where she is; it's not nice, but once she gets used to it, the job becomes interesting, well, a little bit.

The passengers can't see Teresa, they ask nothing from her specifically, but some nights she feels exhausted by their one-way company. On a busy shift with multiple passengers, she is reminded of the stiffness of nights out on the town with coworkers at old temp jobs—office happy hours, someone's birthday. She never had a handle on how to sit at a bar with someone she knows well but who is not a friend, never knew what to talk about. She'd look at her drink and wait for an hour to pass, feeling more lonely and stuck in time and stuck in place than she had ever felt by herself. To drive the CR is to feel like she's forever on the cusp of getting startled by someone else with endless questions: "How's your mother?" "How's your boyfriend?" "What about the Patriots this season?" The constant sense she's bending around to accommodate what others want because her own needs are alien, she never has the language to express her boundaries.

Teresa picks up a man in Auburndale at the start of her shift on a sunny afternoon. Once Teresa, the CR, cruises down the Pike, the man pulls a pistol from his canvas laptop bag. He sits there, perfectly still, back straight, upright in a position that defies the ergonomically perfected curve of the CR seats. His face conveys nothing but blankness. This man, white, thirty-two years old or just about, could be anyone in the city. Teresa envies that. The kind of privacy she has spent her life trying to build, why, this man has it all the time, he gets it automatically.

He is impossible to read, this blank man who believes he is alone, but Teresa imagines he must constantly feel calm and content wherever he goes. That's one of us, Teresa thinks. The gun resting casually on his lap is an unsettling sight, but she realizes he is unlikely to leave much of a mess, which means, weapon or no weapon, this passenger is an ideal one.

The man disassembles the magazine and barrel from the gun. He pulls out a tiny brush on a rod and two swabs, grabs solvent from his bag, and sets out the parts on the white tray table he opened from the side of the seat. Carefully he cleans the pistol. Involved and atten-tive, his ritual reminds Teresa of the woman with the makeup kit she saw in South Station that first week of training. As they cloverleaf from the highway to the Longwood area near the hospital, the man, with a famil-iar grip, puts the gun back in his bag. They stop at an apartment complex near the BU campus.

As she taps for directions to the nearest PUG—a pop-up garage—Teresa wonders if she should be con-cerned about this man who shared space with her, and what he might do with that weapon, but she decides it is not her responsibility to care what happens before and af-ter a passenger enters the car. She was hired to be invisi-ble. That's her real job.

There's a PUG equidistant between the MassTech and Harvard campuses near the business park, with its menagerie of inactive office buildings where no one ever seems to be coming or going. It's a nice PUG. There's a coffee vending machine, the kind that makes a sugary cappuccino that tastes like hot chocolate. Before she can scan her AllCash account for the drink, her phone buzzes with another ride request. She cleans the interior of the car quickly. The gunman didn't leave a mess.

She, the vehicle, pulls up to a freshly painted three-decker with a jungle of plants on the front porch. A cou-ple enters the CR. Teresa listens as they marvel at the technology.

"Incredible. How does this even work?" the woman

says, looking around the carriage for answers, an errant pipe or screw that could explain the magic trick. She has a mahogany red retro helmet of Bettie Page hair and a rockabilly dress printed with cherries showing off a bouquet of cleavage. The boyfriend looks younger, with tattoos up his arms and a flattop. He's wearing one of those oversized bowling shirts with broad stripes on either side. He seems just as confounded and charmed. "Dang," he says, "the future arrived early just for us."

Swing dancers. Their retro-upon-retro styling seems to have been painstakingly selected to evoke mid-century counterculture as revitalized in the 1990s.

The night is clear, and autopilot handles much of the steering. Teresa is reminded of another job she once had, one of the jobs that she usually forgets when she swims in the YMCA lanes. In college, for a semester, she worked as a dishwasher in the cafeteria. Sometimes she'd sneak a glance at the long tables when she passed by the counter to refill the industrial soap. She'd see people she knew. They wouldn't know she was there. Other times, she would wonder who all those people were and try to imagine what their lives must be like from what she could see, from a distance; like one of the lecturers, an old man, sitting alone in the corner with a tiny plate of spaghetti on his tray and a giant slice of chocolate cake.

The CR approaches the bridge on Mass Ave. Cambridge dissolves into Boston with city lights burning at either end and the river dark. Flattop looks out the window and points up at a shimmering skyscraper ahead. "That's the palace of Murata-Carpinelli. All lit up."

"So what? It looks the same at night," Bettie Page–alike says. She remains fascinated by the carriage and the screen and ignores the view when they cross the Charles River. Teresa drops them off at their South End destination. A cabaret revival nightclub. Kind of a new place, it opened when she was living in New York. Every night tourists and theater kids from Emerson line up around the block to get in. She went there once for a college friend's bachelorette party.

Teresa won't remember their faces, but she'll remember their hairstyles. She will remember this drive as one of her first times. She won't remember the building the guy pointed out because she couldn't see it. That part of the couple's conversation will remain a mystery. Maybe he didn't say "palace." Maybe he didn't say "Murata-Carpinelli." Later she will google for hours, spelling "Murata" and "Carpinelli" in all possible variations of consonant letters. Nothing. She will wonder if it's better for her sanity to keep the sound from the carriage off, but for now, the passengers are her connection to the world, even if she cannot engage with them any more than she can with the world.

15

Music is playing in Framingham. It sounds too crisp to be a recording. The traffic at the intersection moves on a green light to reveal across the way a beautiful girl on the curb strip before the Starbucks plaza parking lot playing an electric violin. Her red hair in a frizzy French braid jumps in time with a rock song Teresa can't recognize without the lyrics. There's a guy with her. He's got matching freckles. Probably her brother. Maybe a twin brother. A little taller but not much. The brother is holding a handmade sign with felt marker writing in green and black: "MoM Needs $for SURGERY. Every Bit Helps. GOD BLESS" and a GoFundMe web address. There's an amp in the grass with wires that loop back to a blue pickup in the lot. Clouds above them are heavy and dark with the rain about to fall. The violinist is deep in concentration as her brother waves at the cars that pass. Some honk. Teresa fishes a couple ones from her wallet. She crosses at the intersection by the siblings and drops the cash in an empty coffee can.

Before long, there's some guy in her belly on his phone who needs a ride from an industrial park in Natick to his house ten minutes away. It's easy; afternoons are easy. She turns on public radio. Piping through the nest speakers is the familiar voice of Fal Guidry: "The world has had enough of corporate parasites like Tesla and Uber." He's speaking to the press at the AllOver office in Rome. "They treat your government like it is the enemy and exploit your cash-strapped public services. The era of du-plicitous gig work and self-driving fraud has come to an end with AllOver's CR fleet."

Teresa doesn't know what to make of Falconer Guidry. Usually that means she thinks favorably of someone but doesn't know why. Maybe she should read his book. He's misrepresenting the technology, but for the reasons Philip explained, it does make sense. Boston could be a nice city if it had as few cars as Amsterdam. And she agrees that when it comes to climate solutions, humanity can't wait.

"The CR is truly driverless," Falconer continues. "While our competition builds light-rail-track Pinewood Derby toys, we offer you the first truly fully operational autonomous vehicle. Those other guys, they develop tech-nology the way a con artist thinks: build a distraction and reach for people's pockets. They blindside you with bells and whistles to sell your identity as data. But this project is my commitment to you. We built the CR as public trust. We recognize privacy as a human right. That is why there is no safety driver in the CR."

Well, not quite, Teresa thinks, but at least she has privacy.

"Every other so-called driverless car shuts down in the rain. How is that going to work as climate change continues to upend our everyday lives? I look at this, and every problem, through the lens of the Holistic Apex. Societal problems are interconnected; thus we need systematic solution-making. As democratic institutions fail and the social safety net crumbles under austerity measures, I put forth to the public this, an omni-solution, the CR. A green car, a privacy machine, an end to misinformation, a pledge for justice, rights, and a world in which everyone is your neighbor, your friend, your brother. That's what AllOver offers uniquely as a people-first, community-minded enterprise."

Teresa looks down at the passenger inside who is looking at his phone. No safety driver, but there is safety. She is the good fairy they can't see.

There's a RAV4 on the side of the road and the doors on either side of it are open. Cars ahead of her slow down. Two young men stand on either side and cross each other, in front of the SUV. They wave to the cars in the passing traffic. *It's fine*, they seem to be saying, with their smiles as they wave. *We're just switching drivers.* They don't wave to the CR, although Teresa slowed down just the same. They kiss after they take their seats.

She stops at a red light next to a basketball court in West Roxbury. The teenagers notice the CR, stop their game, and gather around it. One of the kids throws a rock. Another kid throws a bigger rock. She doesn't feel it, but she sees it. She taps on the interior audio while the kids keep throwing rocks at her. The passenger inside the CR doesn't look up from his iPad. He's a few blocks from his house in Chestnut Hill. This is a good neighborhood and those are nice white kids.

There is a call straightaway when she returns to the PUG. A couple leaving the convention center. Maybe not a couple. Two people, in any case, a man and a woman. Could be in private equity or lawyers, they are dressed like it, and both have overnight luggage with them, which appears light, although the man made a show of lifting the woman's suitcase, along with his own, into the car and stowing it in the overhead racks. Teresa set her responder to pass on airport drop-offs, so where are they headed? She glances at the destination on the map: Seaport Hotel. There's construction on the Mass Pike and stop-and-go traffic; what should be a twelve-minute drive is double that. Even with only the back of her head to determine this, it would appear the woman passenger is uncomfortable. She pulls her skirt down to better cover her bare legs and twists in her seat with her knees toward the window. He is talking; she nods and looks out the window. Teresa shuts off her music and turns on the passenger speaker. But the man stopped speaking. Teresa's eyes dart from the road to the view of the passengers. The man has now put his hand on the woman's bare knee that she had been careful to tuck away from him. "Enough," the woman says. "Stop it. Just stop it." He appears to back down, then reaches for her arm and touches her neck. The woman gets up from her seat and moves to the other side of the car, but there is nowhere for her to go; the CR carriage is small. Teresa drops them off at their hotel. She cannot see their faces and wonders if that woman has a room to herself. Teresa can do nothing. She doesn't know who these people are, although the vehicle, and all its sensors, undoubtably recognized them down to the last website they accessed, regardless of what Falconer Guidry said about the privacy policy. This happened while Teresa was never there.

Now she's back around the waterfront with the Children's Museum across the bridge. Ahead is a flock of a dozen wild turkeys strutting with their feathers fanned out. They have taken over a street corner. People are photographing the birds from a distance while a Honda Civic waits for them to pass, holding up traffic. That driver wants to park in the spot that the turkeys have claimed. Teresa can hear cars honk at the driver trying to park. She can't hear the birds gobbling.

16

Three teenage girls ride in Teresa's CR. Sisters or cousins, she guesses. They aren't engaged with one another the way you expect to see among young friends. One of the girls is fidgety in her seat, bobbing her knee up and down and playing with her hair. The girl has the kind of shyness that seems like she has much to say but no idea how to say it and therefore sits silently in frustration. Teresa was like that at that age. She would have liked riding in a CR as a teenager. Or maybe not. Teenager Teresa loved the trains. At the Stoughton commuter rail or the Quincy Adams T, before a trip in town to visit the record shops and thrift in the dollar-a-pound room at Garment District, she delighted in the preview of the city before the city: the commotion on the platform, the rattling sounds of an approaching train car, flashes of city life like trailers before a movie.

It's a short drive on back roads, Lexington to Concord,

and with the lull of activity, Teresa's mind begins to wander. She feels uneasy about what happened in the CR the other night.

"Just. *Stop.*"

Some people know how to intervene. About a year ago, on a near-empty Red Line train, Teresa was reading a book. Another passenger kept looking at her, trying to get her attention with irritating whispery comments: *heyheyheygirlwhatchareadingtellmewhatchareading.* She wondered if he could tell that she was twice his age or if he just didn't care. She kept her eyes on her book and ignored him until he walked over to her. He grabbed the book: *justwantedtoseewhatyouwerereading.*

A voice from the other side of the train car bellowed out, "Don't you touch her!" This man, who had been sitting with a dolled-up blond, got up. Barely south of seven feet tall, this man had as thick an accent as she'd ever heard. "You don't wanna staht trouble. Not with me." His complexion went pink as he glared at the other man. "Ya know what? Get offa the T cahr! When this train stops, I don't wanna see ya, pal." The doors opened at Downtown Crossing and the man who had been harassing her quietly dipped out. Teresa wondered if the bigger man did this in part to show off for his date, but whatever his motivation, he had put a stop to it and she was grateful.

What did she see in the CR carriage last night? Technically, nothing, but she couldn't look away because she didn't believe it would stay that way. She's had those kinds of car rides too. There was that time at the museum job, just before the holiday break, 2015. Her boss talked excitedly about the show he was scheduled to cocurate, *General Strike! May '68 and After.* They shared a taxi on their way back from an opening at another museum. She sensed something was off about his conversation. Then he said, "You know what people are going to think if they see us alone in this cab together, right?"

In the space of seconds, which felt much longer, she discounted her first instincts, to retreat inside her awkward nature and pretend she did not understand. She could reply, cold and dumbly, "What people? Say about what?" It had seemed, even in that instant, too risky to strategize. Teresa asked the driver to pull over and burst out to the curb, shouting that she left something back at the museum before Jord or the driver could say anything. She walked three miles home. The walking and the city at night, freezing and empty under streetlamps, made her feel safe again.

"No. *Stop!*"

Teresa should have stopped the CR. It occurs to her, finally, wilting in traffic, transferring the next passenger from Concord to Mass General, stuck behind a Mack truck with Maine plates. The Mylar in the nest brushes lightly against her bare shoulders. There was something she could have done, in the cold clarity of the moment. She had acted then, as she had felt, that everything was rote and every movement to take had been choreographed in advance. In retrospect, she realizes, there had been options.

"I could have stopped," Teresa says aloud to herself. "The passenger said stop. I could have taken it as directions." She could have, and still, it could keep the illusion true: Wouldn't passengers expect the CR to have speech recognition?

If she had stopped the CR, paused at a street corner, say, with her foot kicked firm on the brake, she would have received a yellow-light warning pulsing in her eyes and an alarm pinging loud in the nest. Aggravating, yes, but something she could have tolerated for five minutes with a sense of purpose. Rose Quartz customers are rich and impatient; they wouldn't wait longer than a minute or two for a defective vehicle to jump-start back to life again. Plus, this act would have prompted unease and a break in the illusion. The man might have pulled back, as the threat of surveillance would have made him feel less sure of himself. He wouldn't have known it was Teresa watching, but even camera eyes repress human behavior. All she had to do that night was put forth the suggestion that he was being watched, and in a manner that was entirely believable. After all, even new economy cars come equipped with smart sensors and dash cams these days.

Just *stop*. You know *what people are going to think*. She remembers the morning after that taxi, when Jord fired off an email that began, "I hope you don't misinterpret what happened last night." When she saw it in her iPhone inbox, she deleted the message without reading it. If she had stayed in the taxi ride, nothing might have happened, probably nothing. Now what she remembers most clearly of that night is the back of the taxi driver's head. Did he hear anything, would he have helped her? The interior of a car is such a small space; how can it fit people who remain strangers?

It took years and two hundred miles before she recognized the power dynamics that fueled her discomfort. Until then, Teresa had room to believe the situation at that job was normal and any problem was her being difficult. Once, after a meeting, he put his hand on her shoulder. Just left it there, his hand centimeters from her neck. When he lifted his hand, she felt the palm print remain like his hand had burned through and left pink marks. Her discomfort with the situation she interpreted as her own regrettably uptight nature. He was the one who was good with people, right? She wondered if she should touch people more in that casual way that other women always seemed to have a handle on. Just lightly tap someone on the forearm when they say something funny. That's what people do to show that they are engaged, don't they? At dinner with a writer, a gay man, a friend at the time but someone she hasn't been in touch with in years, she made a point to tap him on the forearm when he said something funny. She even tapped him on the knees when he made another joke. She felt embarrassed later, unsure whether she felt embarrassed that she was overthinking something that came naturally to everyone else or if it was that she had been uniquely oblivious until then. And if that were the case, what else about life had she failed to understand?

The longer she worked at the museum, the more it felt like training in reverse. Instead of opening up to her, the art world expanded to reveal more ceremonies of human behavior that would forever remain opaque and outside her comprehension. The others all seemed to know the rules of the game, but she was winging it. Sometimes students from good schools would find her work email. "I hope you don't mind this letter out of the blue," began one message. "I strongly admire the material you publish at the Brooklyn Modern. I am a junior year art history student at the University of Chicago and I would appreciate any advice on how to build a career with the leverage of an institution like yours." Teresa found these messages puzzling and unnerving. She never wrote back. More email she deleted.

And sometimes Teresa had been the jerk. She knew this, that she had been, not often but at least once when she worked at the museum. An old friend from Amesfield State said she was in New York for a conference. Colleen Cooke, her roommate freshman year. Teresa had plans to get to an opening that night and told her old friend to meet her at a trendy bar nearby. Teresa arrived with an art world friend and the three had a stilted conversation. She had half a glass of wine and left with her new friend without inviting her old friend along to the gallery where they were headed. Teresa had looked at her old friend, dressed in a heavy marigold-colored sweatshirt with the "GAP" logo embroidered across the front, and she felt embarrassed. Years later, Teresa would dwell on this and her priorities: How could you end a friendship over a sweatshirt? Colleen was your friend. Why did you do that? She'd go over it in her mind at night when she'd brush her teeth and get ready for bed. You weren't kind; Colleen deserves to hate you. She'd never act like that again. It was a comforting thought. Teresa could do better the next time around.

Teresa boarded the wrong train on her way home and discovers her mistake in a sleepy coastal town north of the city. There is nothing but a platform plank at the station. She sits on the curb and waits. On her phone, she pulls up the AllOver home page. She clicks on the "About" section and reads through several pages that declare AllOver's commitment to a "progressive disability-inclusive and diverse financial services community." This leads her to a page that gives the address to AllOver HQ and a phone number.

"Hola, ni hao, bonjour, konnichiwa. Hello, hello! Welcome to AllOver! Just to let you know, this call will be recorded for quality assurance."

Teresa remembers the rules from the lesson in training: be nice, be safe, don't return to a passenger's home. What she's reporting falls under "be nice" and "be safe," right? She wonders if AllOver might take issue with her identifying the passenger by their departure time and destination.

"This is okay because the drop-off isn't someone's house. I can say the drop-off was a public place, the Seaport Hotel, and that I'm calling because I'm concerned I might have observed a situation that AllOver would not condone," Teresa mutters to herself.

"What was that?" says an automated voice. "If you are calling because you need help getting into your AllOver account, say or press one. For information about the Holistic Apex, say or press two."

She looks left and right to see if anyone is around to catch her talking to herself again.

"For everything else, please say or press five."

Even if she had misinterpreted what she saw in the CR the other night, it seems like this is good practice to know how to report what happens in the vehicles. What if she were a witness to a murder? Wouldn't she want to know what the process is like, in advance?

"We have many exciting products and projects at

AllOver, so this could take a while. Usually solutions can be found by visiting our website at forward-slash help."

She listens to several sets of options in the phone tree system until the recorded voice says, "For information about the CR driverless program, say or press seven."

Pressing seven triggers another recorded message. "Luxury, private, the future is all—"

The commuter rail arrives on the other side of the platform. She shouts into her phone as it rattles, "Operator! Operator!"

"What was that? Main menu. If you are calling because you need help getting into your AllOver account, say or press one."

Back at South Station, people stand like chess pieces facing the same direction in staggered distances away from one another. They face the departure board. Teresa finds a spot too. She notices that the final train to Stoughton for the day will arrive in eight minutes and imagines taking it. She'd hop off at that odd Stratford-upon-Avon station, pass the stores that haven't died, closed for the day, and the abandoned building that used to be Cedars. She could turn at the cracked asphalt and down that street, she'd see her parents' old house. It wasn't much bigger than her great-aunt's place. It had always seemed like a normal house before she lived in New York. Only when she came back did she begin to think that maybe it was not so great.

She wishes she could look in her childhood bedroom one last time and search for the letters her father wrote to her every year on her birthday until she was eighteen. On her first day of college, he handed them to her as a present. She opened them irregularly whenever she thought of them. He didn't date the envelopes on the outside, so it was only when she opened them that she could get a sense of the time, like whether the letter he wrote was from 1995 or 1983. Her father's handwriting wasn't great, and his spelling and grammar made her wonder if he had been dyslexic. There wasn't much to the letters, just a reiteration of how proud he was of her and how he hoped she'd go to college. At least that's what she thought when she was still in college. Now she wonders if there had been more to what he had written. But she lost the box of letters somewhere between Stoughton, Amesfield, Boston, New York, and Stoughton again.

With another forty minutes until the next train to Framingham, she stops by the food trucks at the park across the street. There is light rain, but the taco truck awning covers her. She moves closer to the truck so the man behind her will be covered too. Another man arrives and he stands outside the queue the other two have formed. He's getting wet but he doesn't seem to notice. He stands stiff like the rain isn't happening.

The truck takes AllCash but Teresa opens her wallet. She fishes out four singles and a ten.

"You dropped a quarter," the man in the rain says. She looks down at her feet. All mud. "It's right there. Toward the back," he says. She can't see it.

"Right there," he says again. He sounds frantic. Teresa doesn't understand why he cares. She turns around to see him, but from where he stands in the dark, the glare of the light from the truck washes out his features. The man crouches and grabs the quarter, which he finds behind one of the wheels. He hands her the quarter. She brushes it against her jeans and throws the clean silver coin in the taco driver's tip jar.

She can see him now. He looks at his feet. "Do you have anything so I could get some soup?" he asks.

Teresa is startled. Their exchange happened so fast that she hadn't considered why the man was adamant to find the coin that she dropped. She fishes in her wallet and hands him her last dollar. "I'm sorry I don't have more."

She had almost walked away from that quarter. She can be careless too, sometimes. She shouldn't be so careless.

n the middle of a quiet shift, Teresa waits in one of the PUGs now littered over Greater Boston. On the ground, the PUGs look like pint-size, rectangular variations of Render Falls in modules of prism rock, serrated steel, and plastic. Each is hidden in sinewy streets behind DO NOT ENTER signs that deposit into old marshlands, abandoned industrial parks, and dead shopping malls or old mills that have yet to be rezoned.

Teresa pulls up the standard AllOver app on her phone. She has used it for years, and it includes an archive of her transactions with elaborate charts and graphs. She clicks on the trends page. "You're doing terrific! This year your largest regular purchase is [groceries] at [10]% of your income. [Housing] is [0]% of your income. This is an improvement from last year, when [55]% of your income went to [housing]."

The other AllOver app on her phone is for seer drivers

only. It shows her the shifts she's requested and the "flex" shifts open. A map of the region extending north to Portsmouth, west to Worcester, and south to Warwick, Rhode Island, is marked with animated twinkly stars to indicate which areas are currently short-staffed. Seers who travel more than thirty miles for a shift get a bonus, which is also offered when there are spikes in demand for CRs.

On one tab, seers can view their "road to rest" score, which calculates total time driving. Teresa's score is 20 percent, or "excellent." The job really is a lot of time waiting around. She has racked up countless bonuses, sometimes by accident, including the streak bonus, when she worked more than four days in a row, and a holiday bonus, for the full shift she completed on Indigenous Peoples' Day. On the "Your Progress" tab, Teresa can redeem her hours as AllCash points with an additional 20 percent "cash back"; otherwise she receives a weekly direct deposit to her bank from the temp agency, which is still technically her employer.

Teresa clicks through the app, reading the fine print thoroughly, hoping again to find a contact number or a form to send a message to a human at AllOver. When she scans to the bottom of the "Your Progress" tab, she finds a promising link: "Any questions? Click here." It directs her to the AllOver home page. This time, Teresa clicks on the "Help" page, instead of the "About" section.

"Need help? Talk to Sten, our friendly intuitive help agent. Say 'voice' or type 'text only.'"

"Voice," Teresa says, setting her phone to speaker, while glancing out at a narrow eastward-pointing window with a view of the bay. A peppy gender-neutral voice greets her over her phone.

"Hi! I'm Sten, and I come from outer space. On my home planet, there is no war and everybody loves helping everyone else—especially earthlings! Nothing makes me feel warm and fuzzy like recording these conversations for quality assurance. He he he. If it's okay with you, let's continue! What can I help you with today? Say or type!"

Teresa speaks quietly into her phone. "I work for AllOver."

"Hooray! I love our family."

It's dead silent in the PUG and she notices the sound of traffic on 93 and the crashing waves at high tide in the moment before she speaks. "I want to report an incident. It looked like a situation of harassment in the CR vehicle."

"Oh no, harassment. What sort of harassment? Misinformation? Impersonation? Financial abuse? Phishing? Hate speech? Fraudulent transactions? Other?"

"Harassment harassment. In a CR, it was a passenger. Sexual harassment."

"I'm still learning! Can you try that question again?"

She looks at her phone and sees that Sten has posted a smiley emoticon to the screen, which shows a transcript of their conversation. "Can you direct me to the CR department?"

"Isn't the CR the greatest? I can't wait to show my grammy around in the CR when she comes to visit from Planet Holistic Apex. Are you a Rose Quartz customer? Do you need help requesting a ride?"

"Uh, yes."

"Please enter your RQ number."

The next passenger boards at Newbury Street and Mass Ave. Upon seating, the woman dumps the contents of her Neverfull tote on the floor. Tampons, energy bars, diamond hoop earrings, pens, candy wrappers and used tissues, and hand sanitizer form a pile beside an index card–size Moleskine notebook. One of the earrings rolls from the pile to the crevice near the door. When they get to her destination in Malden, the passenger scoops up her belongings and leaves her trash behind. Teresa wonders if the passenger will forget the hoop, but she picks it up on her way out.

The Seer-CR app shows the GPS locations of truck drivers who work with AllOver logistics partners. You can hail a ride from them if your destination is along the driver's journey. Teresa has tried it a few times and it has always been a welcome awkward connection, a buffer of human contact. It's a chance to be human with someone who doesn't judge her for being no good at it. Sometimes a smile, sometimes a trickle of conversation. Tonight, it will be her first real encounter with another person besides her mother in over a week.

Beside the PUG recharge stations, which turn on automatically when the vehicle is parked and make small repetitive poot sounds, and the robot arm draped in multicolored wires, which transports the seer in and out of the nest, there is a covered platform that looks like a facsimile subway stop. That's where seers wait for their own pickup. Sometimes when she arrives in a PUG, the app will automatically call a truck driver to drop her off at another more in-demand location, say from Canton to Newton. Philip had said it works similar to what happens with pilots at airports. They get flown to other airports often because of regional discrepancies between airplanes and people to fly them. Teresa liked hearing this comparison, that she was doing honorable service, like a pilot, with passengers to watch over. And aren't pilots invisible to passengers just like she is?

She waits outside the PUG under a black-ultramarine sky in the tranquil parking lot of the abandoned East Anchorway motel near Revere Beach and Wonderland. It might be Deer Island that she sees as faint lights in the water. Behind her, high beams from an incoming driving giant cut the darkness. Light shines toward her like unblinking eye contact. She returns to the PUG to catch her ride.

"Tough night," the driver says, as she enters the vehicle with a leaping step up to the passenger seat.

"I can imagine," she says. "Gotta be tiresome going such long distances. How do you do it?"

"Talking 'bout you. Tough night for you?"

"Could be worse," Teresa says quietly. "Some things in those cars, I'd rather not see." She realizes she is talking like a mysterious hitchhiker in an old horror movie from the eighties and laughs. "But it's a job, y'know."

18

A man in Dedham has requested a lift all the way to T. F. Green International outside Providence. Teresa would not have accepted this passenger ordinarily.

Some of the seers prefer the route to the airport and take the requests back and forth again and again. She tried it once, but Teresa found it too hectic. The tunnel to Logan is overwhelming with all the lights, and the signage to terminals with various airline names listed on them made her doubt her sense of direction. And once she got there, she had to pass through the dedicated rideshare waiting area in the basement of the labyrinthine parking garage by Terminal E to meet the passengers. It's the one preference she has set up in the app: no airport drop-offs. This excludes all regional and municipal airports too.

This passenger had originally requested a trip to the Pilgrim Square Mall in Attleboro. It struck Teresa as incredibly strange. That mall, as she understands it, is practically dead. No Waldenbooks, no Express, no Chess King, no Wilsons Leather, no Payless, no Radio Shack or Cedars or Ritz Camera. There's a JCPenney and a Macy's and a black hole in the center of three floors and eight hundred square feet of commercial space. Why would this guy want to go there. And all the way from Dedham, too.

He didn't want to go to the Pilgrim Square Mall in Attleboro. Inside the CR, once they hit I-95, the passenger changed his destination to T. F. Green.

This airport is nowhere near as chaotic as Logan, but the passenger is unruly. When she stops curbside at arrivals, the passenger refuses to exit. Cars behind her honk. She closes the doors. Teresa follows exit signs and circles around again as the passenger types something into his phone. Again, she attempts to drop him off at arrivals. He refuses to exit again.

"Oh, c'mon," she says to herself. He's being selfish. Yes, you can be selfish to driverless technology, Teresa decides.

The passenger barks into his phone about the trouble he's having with the CR vehicle. An AllOver operator tries to set him straight. "Sir, it's not up to me. I can't authorize this. We are appreciative of your loyalty as a neighbor and shareholder, but the CR has a limited service radius. It's for your own safety."

While he talks, Teresa circles around the traffic island

at arrivals. There's a guy on a motorcycle coming up from her blind spot and she almost crashes into him.

"Sir, these boundaries are not arbitrary but held up through geofencing. The CR isn't equipped to drive outside the mapped area."

The man waves his fist in the air and shouts into his phone, "This is an emergency! My wife is pregnant and I am urgently needed at our Narragansett residence."

The operator asks him to hold. "We have a PickUp waiting for you at T. F. Green. At no expense to you. Obviously this lacks the superior technology and private luxury of the CR, but it is the best human-operated ride service in the business. Sound good?"

Finally the selfish passenger gets out.

She ends her shift in time for the first Framingham commuter rail of the day. At the station, amid weary early-morning travelers clutching giant coffees from Dunkin' and Sundry Meadows, she sits before the live TV screens. The one tuned in to CNBC is playing loud. "AllOver is set to join the S&P 500 index next month after six quarters of record-making earnings. Shares surged to an all-time high following the announcement yesterday morning."

Teresa looks up at the Bethany-like announcer providing these details on the TV screen as the ticker OVAA and its price glides through the chyron in bright green letters and numbers. "AllOver has operated at major losses for most of its sixteen-year history, but no one can deny that this has been a breakout year for the Redwood City–based fintech juggernaut. Bolstered by the success of the CR driverless program and the 'AllCool' teen payment app, the stock has rallied three hundred percent since February and it shows no signs of slipping as active portfolio managers add shares to their funds that track the S and P. CEO and founder Falconer Guidry has a vision and with this news, he has a mandate from shareholders."

"The CR is impressive. I tried it out the first time last week," says one of the commentators. "And it has to be the most iconic-looking vehicle since the Volkswagen Bug. Such a bright and fun design. Real fun and it's good for the environment too."

There is footage of a press conference from the previous day. A reporter asks Falconer, "How would you respond to Senator Loomis and Senator MacIntyre, who argue that your company should be broken up?"

"Antitrust is a pro-capitalist policy," Falconer answers serenely. "The framework is designed to encourage competition and the preservation of the free market. Now, competition is fine when we are talking about a game of gin rummy. But if tiny decentralized factions controlled our water supply and means tested it, this would lead to society's ruin. As I explain in my book, *Holistic Apex*, decentralization is antidemocratic—that's what antitrust legislation gets us. AllOver is public innovation delivered with the efficiency and speed of the marketplace. We believe in solidarity, public trust, and mutual aid as enterprise."

The reporter looks baffled by the AllOver founder's words. "Feels like you're conflating users and constituents, and maybe shareholders too?"

"Yes, and underlying this difference is the cult of individualism. Look, let me take you back to why I founded AllOver and what motivated me. I built my business for people who know what it's like to get a medical bill you can't pay or when a credit card goes into collections and they're calling you on the hour at home and at work. Do you have any idea what that's like? A menacing voice says he knows where your girlfriend lives and he'll pay her a visit if you don't cut a check right now. I know these things."

Teresa is surprised by how naturally Falconer transitions from corporate-speak to flustered sincerity. She walks closer to the television screen to better hear what he's saying.

"America needs trusted institutions. Capitalism has failed the twenty-first century just like communism failed the twentieth. We need real alternatives: progress for the people, climate justice, freedom from tyranny. I understand the public distrust in the technology sector. My neighbors in Silicon Valley, the tech elite, they built their empires as thieves: gorging on your personhood as data."

The AllOver founder pauses and smiles warmly. "And I see a similar flawed mindset from the neo-Luddites and critics of platform capitalism. It would appear that every one of them went to Harvard and has rich parents. In academic journals they talk of economic exploitation and class struggle, but I know these people. None of them acknowledged my existence until I made my first million. They call themselves socialists, but I know this well: they won't look you in the eyes unless you are rich just like them. What I believe is the Holistic Apex. I work with and for the people but especially those that the Silicon Valley elite exploit and the neo-Luddite elite look down upon. I will never forget where I came from."

Teresa knows how rhetoric works and has a rough sense that anything the founder says comes from market research and has been coached to perfection with the help of the world's best-paid publicists. Still, she is moved to see a person in power speak candidly like this.

Falconer reminds her of someone she knew at Mass-Tech, the job she took a few years out of college, a couple years before the recession hit. "If you told anyone that there's a city where every August, all the world's most self-important eighteen-year-olds descend on it, they invade it, people would think you're crazy. But that's what happens here," Kieran told her. It was her third day on the job. All the administrative staff from departments and admissions had met at an ice cream social on the front lawn to celebrate a longtime admissions staffer's retirement.

Kieran never set out to be an admissions officer. He applied online for a role as a "Communications Specialist." The school provided only a vague job description on purpose. "List it on Monster dot com and insane mothers in Newton would flood the application portal." Fifteen minutes into the interview, the staff told him what he was really there for: they needed somebody to take a close look at applicants with music backgrounds. He played piano in state-level competitions and tutored junior high school music students. It was on his résumé, that's why they called him. Now he's a voting member in the final admit meetings.

"They're all alike by the time I'm looking at them. Perfect SATs, straight As. Some admissions staff try to make a science out of it, but they're all alike. All elite. And alike, as in, anyone who applies to a school like this would shove a baby for a lifeboat off the *Titanic*. I do my part to raise my hand as randomly as possible. I can make a case for anyone. All I have to say to justify any vote is that the candidate demonstrates leadership. See, if I actively tried to undermine the system, I would end up with my own set of criteria and objectives. It's more subversive not to care either way; treat it like the stupid lottery it is."

Teresa was baffled by the rigmarole that Kieran described. "What's 'demonstrates leadership' even mean?"

"It's what you do to get into these schools. Say there's an open 'student rep' position on the school committee at your high school. No one wanted to do it and your guidance counselor says, 'Oh, you really should. It will look great on your CV.' You take it, and it's basically sitting at a desk with the grown-ups talking about line items in student lunch budgets on the first Thursday night of every month. In your application, which I see, you stress the importance of the role of a student rep. You probably imply that you won an election for this position even though it was handed to you. Then say something like, 'I advocated for youth as a leader in my community.' That's demonstrating leadership. It's the bullshit. They all do it and they keep doing it through college too. These people only stop demonstrating leadership once they attain power of some sort—tenure-track professorship, whatever. Leader-led leadership—you're no longer just demonstrating it."

Kieran looked out at the field. "You went to Amesfield, right?" He had a light lilt-y accent coming and going. His parents, she imagined, might be recent immigrants or maybe they had those inexplicable Boston accent variations that sounded Irish, with that speed and intonation and murmured pinch-vowel rhythm even if they'd themselves never set foot on the island nor had any family members of theirs since the famine.

"I didn't get in anywhere else," Teresa said.

"Got a lot of Amesfield folks in admissions. I went to

Hawksboro State," he said. "It's all you need, really. The way it works in Canada is you write down your grades in pencil and send that in with a self-addressed stamped envelope. In Canada, everyone goes to Canadian Amesfields and UMasses. Keeps the country sane. Notice they got a functioning government."

"I guess I just didn't care that much when I was in high school," Teresa said. It's true. She didn't. She checked out the well-worn copy of the *American Complete Guide to Colleges and Universities* in the high school library that was five years out of date and had tomato sauce stains over the section on UMass. She flipped through pages and descriptions for various schools and paused on some of the weirder names, like Harvey Mudd and Case Western, wondering what their deal was, but every school seemed the same. Some were more expensive, but how different could they be? School is school.

Teresa could see part of the Charles River from the picnic table where they were sitting. The MassTech campus was stark. There weren't many trees, not even on the lawn where the staff had gathered. With its limited canopy coverage, this part of Kendall Square—once a salt marsh—still looked, in those years, like an industrial city. Now it's an average of eight grand a month for a studio apartment.

"Scholarship kids are the worst. Don't be shocked," he said. "They keep the racket going. Let's say the roulette wheel spins for me. I get into Princeton, make my dad proud. First year, I think I don't deserve it. Someone made a mistake. The other students, oh, they're so much more cultured and sophisticated than me. Sophomore year, I internalize the difference. Start thinking, I'm the only one here who deserves the honors. I worked hard, they had it easy. By senior year, the institution has me inside out. Start thinking, I'm a force of nature and I know what's best for the world. From my corner office at Raytheon, Exxon, Bear Stearns, I believe I can change the system from inside it, when in fact the whole time I've been its mark. For the rest of my life, I'll think I'm not like them, but I will be." Kieran looked down Mass Ave and nodded his head in the direction of the other good school. "That's the Big H mindset, especially."

The Harvard campus, Teresa did not like. Old brick buildings, imposing and colonial, fortressing the people there away from everyone else in Cambridge. Sometimes Teresa would see young women her age in the vintage shops that she went to and drinking coffee at locally owned cafés that she liked. But she could always tell that they were different. The Harvard students carried themselves different.

"Harvard is a hedge fund first and a system to identify and isolate the ruling class second. They come to Boston for four years, fail to make a single friend from BU or BC. And forget Bunker Hill Community College. Whatever capacity they had to connect in a meaningful way to the ninety-nine point nine nine nine nine

nine nine percent of the non-Harvard universe is destroyed by the time they graduate." Kieran jammed at the last of his Hoodsie cup with its flat wooden spoon. "The Ivy League is Scientology for people in Weston, Bethesda, Westchester County. At least with the Russell Group, there's a sort of pessimistic sense of determinism to it all. But here, despite all the 'demonstrating leadership' bullshit, they believe in it, because it affirms them as the righteous."

Teresa shook her head. It wasn't that Kieran was bothering her exactly, but she felt like he was ranting at her about something she didn't understand. "Don't you worry about reading too much into this?"

"It's my job. I find it so interesting it makes me sick."

After decades of precarious employment, Teresa has come to sympathize with Kieran's rage. A small part of it. She feels it in twinges of resentment, especially at the ends of temp contracts. It is a spark that can burn in her, something she is careful to extinguish quickly and offer no kindling or else she'd see nothing and have nothing but that fire in her. She felt it driving Vermont Qualline around Stoughton. How could Falconer work with someone like that?

On the screen, Falconer continues to engage with the press, including a question about his ultimate goal for the CR program. "The CR is a systemic solution to a crisis that the public sector cannot be mobilized to resolve alone. That is, the problem of too many cars on the road, their climate-ravaging impact, and city planning that is hostile to pedestrians and cyclists."

A CR parks behind Falconer. The doors switch open.

"If you have problems with AllOver or the Holistic Apex, I am happy to field them anytime," Falconer shouts as he enters the vehicle. "But this vision is bigger than me. I am a humble public servant to all nine billion people around the globe. Remember that when we win, you win with us!"

Teresa does have a problem and she would like to talk to him. She has another idea now, and enters a search on her phone: "allover staff help line."

A human answers it. "AO ID number?"

"I don't think I've got one."

"It's the number on your computer."

"I don't have a computer."

"Are you a contractor?"

"Yes."

"Sorry, this is AO only. Contact your staffing agency with any questions."

Teresa watches the OVAA stock price pass on the chyron once more as the CNBC anchor repeats her report.

19

Teresa finds the Render Falls training director on LinkedIn. He's based in Milwaukee, but he's conducting another "workshop series" in Miami at the moment. "Sorry to bother you," she says in the message she sends to Philip. "I have a question about the CR program and I have no idea who to get in touch with about it." There has to be some kind of help line for seers, she thinks, and he, if anyone, would know the process for it.

She's off to pick up her first passengers that shift: four guys leaving a MassTech dormitory and headed to Providence. She misses her job at MassTech. It was the one job she had that her father took any interest in. He said that universities have some of the best benefits and pensions around. "When you're older, you'll come to appreciate that."

MassTech wasn't fancy inside, at least not in the

corridors where she roamed. The floors were gray and beige, but the ceilings were high and the windows were narrow and tall. The place reminded her of the corridors in her high school, and she wondered if it was because both places made her feel small. After work, she'd swim in the Olympic-size pool in what was the nicest gym she'd ever seen.

Teresa makes her way through one of the more Lovecraftian streets in a town complete with austere old houses painted in jewel tones vivid under the overcast late-afternoon sky. Four young woman are seated on the porch of a forest green and mulberry Victorian with gingerbread-style detailing. She parks and the guys get out. One of the young women calls to them, "Nice ride!"

When she worked at MassTech, she went out a few times with some of the grad students, but every time, eventually, she'd find out they had girlfriends at Brown or Amherst College. Or Wellesley and Brandeis, just outside the city, which to a twenty-four-year-old might have felt like long distance. Sinisa was different.

Early on, right after they met, she'd sit on the floor at Borders and flip through the world atlas to look at maps of the Balkans region. And whenever there was a newspaper left in the break room, she'd open up the International section and check to see if there was anything there about Serbia and the neighboring region.

Sinisa would hang around the doorframes after department meetings and wait for her as she printed out expense reports for the senior administrative assistant or correspondence that she had ghostwritten for one of the professors. A lanky guy with a blond ponytail practically swimming in his oversized T-shirts. He was so bony it startled her at first. His elbows and kneecaps felt like lug wrenches, but it was not unattractive. Just different. Not what she was used to. Before her lunch breaks, Sinisa would ask to go with her and he'd sit there across the table outside with a deli sandwich all quiet, just smiling. It's not like he would have been much of a talker if he wasn't a little embarrassed about his English, but there were long pauses and silences, not uncomfortable; just space in the relationship to be filled, which they filled with movies.

"We should do something. Not just sit in a cold room in front of a screen," he said, after they took their seats in a movie theater. They had gone to see *Elevator to the Gallows*. It was the second film they had seen in the basement of the Coolidge Corner Theatre just that week. "Maybe . . ." She tried to think of a place farther south than Stoughton but not too far and not too fancy. "Fall River?" With a rental car, they drove down to tour the old battleship at Battleship Cove. They spent the night at the Borden House on Second Street, as in Lizzie. Sinisa didn't know who that was when he booked the room. Just that the building had history involving a crime and a woman.

Sinisa took off his sunglasses and glanced up at the Borden House with its green-black shingles and black-black shutters. The place looked like someone put their teenage goth daughter in charge of exterior remodeling. "It's feminist, this house?"

"I'm not sure either," Teresa said.

They toured the place after they checked in. The tour group included a number of middle-aged women with short hair and baggy sweatshirts. Behind them, lingering shyly like fawns, stood their teenage daughters—adorable girls in plastic corsets and fishnet sleeves and cake eyeliner, teetering in off-brand Fluevogs. "I don't think she did it," one of the girls said quietly from behind her mother in the back as they all stood in the bedroom where the alleged murderess used to sleep. Teresa looked at the girls and noticed she lingered around Sinisa the same way.

Their room was under a slanted roof. Sinisa had to cross over the bed to get to the other side because of how the ceiling narrowed. They had been walking all day, and when she got to the bed she felt a sense of relief in her legs and a completeness with Sinisa beside her. There was nothing to do in the room but lie on the bed and talk— quietly, for rustling from the other rooms could be heard in theirs and they didn't wish to be heard by others. When Sinisa shut the door, it felt like their room was the entire world and everything beyond the walls had dissolved. If she were to look out the window, Teresa was sure, she'd see nothing but black sky and stars.

They spent every weekend together that summer and then every day. She could walk to work, after that.

Friday afternoon has transitioned into Saturday morning and she's driving her final passenger for the day. It's an elementary-school-aged boy sitting in the CR all alone. She picked him up from a town house across from the L Street Beach in Southie. His mother helped him in the CR and handed him a lunch box and a full backpack. Teresa drops the boy off at an apartment complex in Belmont where his father has been waiting for him in the front lot. Teresa wonders if she'll pick him up again on Sunday night.

Teresa listens to a WGBH segment about private beaches in Massachusetts. Only a tenth of the coastline is open to the public. She wonders if she'll get to see any private beaches when she picks up a passenger.

Back in the PUG she checks LinkedIn on her phone. Philip hasn't written back. She tries to check his profile. He's blocked her.

20

Back in Brixboro, Teresa wakes up to the sound of her neighbors down the street that she has never met. "Mochi! Mochi!" She can hear the elderly couple bang on pots and cry out for their pet. "Mochi! Where are you? Mooochiiii!"

She wonders if she should help them, but their voices grow fainter, indicating to her that they have continued their search in the woods in their backyard. And she's groggier than normal. A cricket made its way inside the house the night before and sang uninterrupted until dawn, voicing its frustration about the situation, which Teresa shared.

Today is her day off and she has made no plans. Her thoughts race back to that unpleasant situation she observed in the CR earlier that week. Part of her brain is trying to convince the other part that what she witnessed was some kind of lovers' quarrel. You never know what two people are like when they're alone together. It's none of her business. The disgust about it that she still feels, well, that's her projecting. Teresa wishes she had a more concrete allegation to report. Something black and white and unmistakably one thing and not possibly interpreted as another. Her difficultly reaching a human being at AllOver amplifies her unease with the situation.

She stretches her legs before getting up from the daybed. The area behind her knee throbs with tension built up from weeks of rush hour stop-and-go braking. Why does she want to call? Someone with concern for others would get up and out and help her neighbors find their cat. What information is she trying to un- earth through this quest? To be honest, she thinks, she'd like to report the incident to voice her own discomfort. Yes, she might have shut off the sound and video feeds from the carriage, but a nagging sense of uncertainty would have gnawed away at her. Yes, she cares about the other woman and hopes her night was safe. But also, yes, the invisible woman was an injured party too. It was painful for Teresa to observe. Intrusive memories of Jord and the museum have cluttered her mind since it happened.

Teresa looks at the website set up specifically for the CR program. There is a phone number listed. This must have been what the Narragansett-bound man had called. "Are you experiencing a CR delay? Have issues with your ride? Contact us." Teresa dials the number.

The operator complains that Teresa is breaking up. "I can barely hear you." Teresa is embarrassed and worries that the operator can tell, from her staticky cell reception, that the house where she lives is not a nice one. "I'm sorry, I'm trying to find more bars." Teresa steps outside. "Is this okay? I'm a seer. I drive CRs."

"What?" The representative snorts. "Think you're confused, ma'am. This line is for passengers for our driverless car program, CR. We do not have drivers."

Teresa tries to explain over the operator's laughter and through the terrible reception. "A seer. I went through training at the New England headquarters in Stoughton, Mass."

"Ma'am. We are talking about driverless vehicles. If you are calling for reasons other than to request a CR pickup, I will have to end this call."

"Okay, I could meet anyone from AllOver at the Framingham Pop-Up Garage in twenty minutes. I'm just trying to report an incident."

"RQ number?"

After hanging up, Teresa feels unsatisfied with what feels like the inevitable conclusion. She knows she's not stupid, but it's easier to pretend otherwise a lot of the time. It is bullshit, this company, the CR program. It's all lies, she knows this and thinks this as she opens a Shawmut Bank statement that arrived yesterday in the mail. But the account balance Teresa sees printed on the page, that's all real.

Teresa grabs her tote bag and walks down the hill to Main Street. The center is a strip of grass with a rotting gazebo before the freshly painted white and stately town hall. It had been a Unitarian church and the steeple is the tallest point in town. On either side of the park are nine storefronts, including an Italian grocery and a Brazilian missionary church in what used to be a shoe store, or at least, that's what the faded mural of an oxford shoe above the awning suggests. Every other shop is empty with a sign in the window with phone numbers in block letters for commercial real estate agents. Rows of three-decker apartment homes in peach and brown and mint-gray and teal crawl up the hills from the town center. You can't see, from this distance, the busted doors, yards littered with broken toys and legless lawn chairs, dirty shutters and window screens with runs. From here, the houses look fit for princes and elves. It is all sherbet houses and Neapolitan ice cream at this vantage point or from the perspective of a driver going twenty-five with their eyes on the road.

Behind the Brixboro library is the YMCA. She pays for a day pass in AllCash, changes into her swimsuit, covers her face lightly with olive oil, and raises her eyebrows before pressing the mirrored goggles to suction around her face.

In the water, cold and familiar, she finds the habit as she used to, counting her life year by year, lap by lap.

Teresa might have stayed at MassTech forever, but

there was another good job. Lap twenty-nine, her first temp contract in New York. She was originally hired for a three-month data entry stint working on spreadsheets and indexes of archival material for a museum's website. Roz, her boss, told Teresa she got her start at MoMA in the 1960s. A receptionist at the time, she made friends with other museum staff like Lucy Lippard (then a librarian), Robert Ryman (security guard), Dan Flavin (art handler), Fred Watts (another security guard), Sol LeWitt (bookstore cashier), and other legends in their cold-water-flat years. They took these jobs to be close to the art. Roz had two small dogs and an apartment by the park with large windows and paintings from her friends on every wall. Her life was, in Teresa's mind, an apex, an absolute ideal—a future both modest and exciting, accessible and right. Hers was a future that Teresa would have liked, and a future that seemed within reach. It didn't feel greedy to want that kind of life.

In three short months, Teresa learned to call shows "exhibitions" instead of "exhibits," what a "biennial" or "biennale" was and how to pronounce it either way.

"Want to know something funny about this place?" Roz said to Teresa on her first day, with that dry voice of hers. "It's not much of a museum at all. There is no permanent collection. You'll find art people don't care much about technicalities." Roz explained that the institution dressed itself up as something bigger, investing in publications, artist monographs in expensive paper, and web content—much of it the materials that Teresa assisted Roz in producing.

Roz once asked her, "Do you have a book that you've never read but feel proud to own? Were you proud to buy that book?" Teresa thought about the set of *Kristin Lavransdatter* paperbacks that she got at Porter Square Books the year before. She had yet to crack them open but packed the books carefully in a box then in her new kitchen in Morningside Heights, still unpacked. She also bought *Lanark* for Sinisa, in that same bookstore visit. All their books were stowed in the same unpacked boxes. Neither of them has read it, but yes, she felt really smart when she brought those books to the register. "That's what publicity is all about and what we do, in our own way. The publications are part of the spell that the museum casts over the public. People feel good about knowing what happens here."

When her three-month contract was up, Roz hired Teresa in a newly created "Content Specialist" post. The job was largely administrative, with some web copy and website maintenance, but Teresa read *October* magazine on her lunch breaks in order to at the very least understand the jargon that Roz worked to avoid. "I want you to read this and tell me what you think of it," Roz said one day, handing her proofs for a forthcoming artist monograph. The next morning, Teresa emailed six hundred words of clean copy summarizing the artist's work and the author's findings, ending with her opinion in brief:

"The artist aims to interrogate the natural world and the man-made to suggest that the line between nature and architecture is ambiguous." Roz invited her to contribute to the magazine and catalogs published by the museum. She taught her how to edit. Teresa, on her own, launched a series of artist interviews for the museum's fledgling weblog. Through Roz, and through her self-motivated study of it, she came to love art. When she explored exhibition floors on her breaks, she had a sense of seeing inside another person's mind, and all they were feeling and motivated to achieve in the construction of each work. Even the work that stumped her never failed to fascinate her.

Like Fred Watts. Teresa confessed, she did not understand what his work was all about. "It just looks like white paint in a frame to me." She could say these things to Roz. She could be honest with her.

They had met that morning at Roz's apartment to have breakfast and sort through boxes of archival papers. Teresa looked at the painted white, seemingly utterly plain canvas that Roz kept on a wall separate from the rest of her collection.

"Look at the way the frame casts shadows on the wall," Roz said. "See how the picture hangs in a certain way because of the canvas? Look at the nails. You can feel the smooth texture of the hardware in contrast with the canvas just by looking at it, right? He's playing with all the elements that make a painting; everything that seems to disappear when we focus on the image. He's showing us the foundation: the shadows from the frame and textures of material and the way something catches light when it is hung in a room. Now can you see it?"

Teresa looked at her feet and shook her hands and wiggled her fingers. She faced the canvas again. She could see it. The plain white paint in a frame had come into focus for her as something otherworldly; a power, almost like kindness, that the artist had shared with her, even if not for her specifically.

"He was really just a security guard when you met him?"

"He was. Seemed to happen more regularly back then. People working their way up from the mail room and that sort of thing."

When Teresa felt overwhelmed with email and invoices, she would get up from her dusty cubicle desk covered in decades of old stacks of papers—stacks that began with Roz's previous assistants, which Teresa worried she shouldn't disturb—and take a walk through the galleries downstairs with spotless white floors in clear-as-day light. Her mind would reset as she considered the colors and the angles and the mass of, say, a Phyllida Barlow sculpture.

Sometimes she felt out of place. A coworker made a joke about moving into a "double-wide" on what the museum paid them. She thought she knew what that was, but she wasn't entirely sure, and looked up the word on

Google Image Search. The pictures that came up all looked like normal houses.

A year in, Roz surprised Teresa with a raise and a new title: "Managing Editor." The salary was the same as what she made in her final year at MassTech. A good salary.

The path cleared for her had appeared simple before: marry Sinisa, have a kid or two or three, follow him wherever he goes, as she did for his Columbia postdoc, and as she had expected to for his upcoming position at a research lab in Pasadena. She had wanted from him all she wanted from anyone: to tell her what to do and leave her alone. Then it happened that she wanted something more; with her promotion, the path had split. She was a career woman with career woman responsibilities and career woman objectives. There were career woman sacrifices that she had to make. It was sad, but also delicious, to say goodbye to him and prioritize her own life before anything else, including this man who she thought she needed to be with when her path had only one direction to travel on. Sinisa bought a car in New Jersey and drove to California alone with their dog.

Teresa moved to a micro-studio in Prospect Heights. It was a place of her own and for the first time. Yes, the bathroom down the hall was shared by all six tenants on her floor, but she never had to learn their names or what they fixed for breakfast or when they ate it. She could smile politely and shut the door and release herself from the expectations of everyone else. She could walk to work.

She started seeing Lance in IT. It didn't last long but he was nice. Several years before, he had volunteered in Central Park to help set up *The Gates* for Christo and Jeanne-Claude. It was winter. He'd just arrived from Atlanta; bought his first warm jacket in his life. Picked up some gloves at Macy's on his way to meet the other volunteers. Lance told her about *The Gates* to explain how he met some people who got him the job at the museum, but she was struck by how easy it happened. She often thinks, with envy, of what it must have been like to be part of the event. He could seal himself inside this public memory, have a personal claim to it. Someone might say, "Remember those orange flags in the park in 2005?" "Yeah, I helped put them up," he could say. Nothing that she had a hand in at the museum felt like that at all. People had to come to the Brooklyn Modern. It wasn't out in the world for the world to see and remember; what they did wasn't for everybody.

In 2014, Roz announced her retirement. Teresa was a candidate to replace her, but the board wanted new blood, a "fundraiser type." Her boss was hit by a car while cycling shortly after her last day. But before all this, it was a good job. The best one.

21

Out in the world hidden like a fly on the wall, like an invisible cloak, like all matters of invisible things described, in idioms, as desirable states, she is learning what other people are like when they think they are alone. Sometimes they shout and cuss at their phones and make faces and stretch their legs.

Teresa requests night shifts; the work is straightforward, the traffic is minimal, and most of the passengers watch the screen and pull out the waffle-knit blankets AllOver provides that are stored under the seats like the vehicle is a mobile extension of their own living rooms. The downside is the night passengers who are messy are very messy. She tries to avoid any requests on the campuses: too often the students squeeze in clown car–style in crowds of eight or nine, and even in groups of three or four at least one is likely to vomit. And night shift passengers are more likely to have sex in the carriage, which is unpleasant to observe and to be near. When it happens, Teresa turns the sound off and the video to the carriage unit off and keeps her eyes on the road and thinks of nothing but overpasses, underpasses, and the directions she has to follow.

Maybe she's nocturnal by nature, or maybe she isn't; the wound-back dramatic shift to her internal clock has unleashed in her a productive derangement. Time itself takes a new, disorienting dimension. Tuesday afternoon is her Sunday morning now that she works weekends and nights. Her body responds to Tuesday afternoon differently. It has taken traits of Sunday: the stability of pancakes, no news, and a near-empty email inbox. She yearns for more people out in the world slowed down like she is on a Tuesday but even here in sleepy rotting Brixboro, people are on their phones on Tuesday, honking their horns on Tuesday; they have places to go, immediately, on Tuesday.

A number of executives use CRs to get to work. Those drives are the most relentless: stop and go, lending to friction in her wrists and tension headaches. Boston is a hospital town, but there are surprisingly few passengers in scrubs; she's driven only one medical worker, in her first two months.

What did she get with her first paycheck? Some necessities at Rite Aid and she paid off a medical bill that had gone into collections. The funds cleared instantly. It felt like shaking off bricks. Afterward she booked a dentist appointment for the first time in two years.

Sometimes she is afraid in the nest, aware of its claustrophobic dimensions, but looking out at the world through the screens at her control center distracts her from this distress, and if that fails, remembering the money always quiets the fears. The fear only comes when she is parked or waiting for a passenger; on the road, she is tuned in and focused; the driving experience is meditative, second nature, just like regular driving.

On the fourth Thursday of November, none of her family is awake or living to celebrate with, so she works all day. She drives a couple with climbing gear to Quincy Quarries, admiring the giant flat rocks tagged with four decades of layers of spray paint as she circles the CR around to the other side of Blue Hills. Sometime later a family requests a CR to drive around Whalesborough to look at Christmas lights. It is a tricky assignment, and hard on her knees—stop and go, stop and go—every five minutes, someone taps to stop, but she likes the family. They carried cups into the CR and share hot chocolate from a thermos. She feels warm with these passengers, watching over them, they are cozy under the blankets, pointing out the window, and sharing with one another this new update to what appears to be a long-running family tradition.

On Christmas, early evening, she picks up a family at the Wang Theatre who had gone to see *The Nutcracker*.

Two little girls in matching red and green jacquard skirts get out of their seats and kick off their patent leather Mary-Janes. They dance on tiptoes, in their stocking feet, white tights dirty and bunched at their ankles, twirling like the ballerinas they had just seen. Their father begins to scold them, but their mother laughs and claps. He lets them carry on with the pirouettes. Teresa drives very carefully. The girls keep their balance as the CR twists and turns and enters the Pike to deliver them home to Sherborn.

Over New Year's, the passengers are less messy than she had dreaded. She emerges, on her break, with her head heavy with memories of times she would be out with them, weaving in and out of house parties from Watertown to Brighton, feeling the excitement from others out on the streets, that the address someone ultimately headed to didn't matter, everyone out there was at the same party. It's pouring outside, washing the last year away. In the rain, she's a stowaway. A teenage runaway floating to Niagara in a barrel. Round and round, in city lights and city traffic. It feels dangerous in a way her life has never been. Inside the CR, as a seer, *seeing*, under the chain mail, wrapped like candy in space blankets, she falls into a trance with a God's-eye view on the rich strangers.

Clasped in the carriage arch with her hips and ribs hugging the half moon cushion, she drives up to the Coolidge Corner Theatre to pick up the next passengers. It is a couple. Ten minutes to Jamaica Plain. Easy. She has the passenger audio on, but they aren't talking. They sit at a distance from each other and stare out opposite windows. Doesn't look good. They might break up in the CR. No one sits like that with someone they want to go home with. Teresa feels relieved when they finally get out. If they break up, they will break up somewhere other than inside her belly. It's not her fault what happens next. It is not her responsibility. The CR cuts through puddles flashing reflections from the streetlights and Christmas lights down Hancock Street that haven't been taken down yet.

It's snowing lightly. The nest is insufficiently heated, and it is just cold enough to feel uncomfortable inside. Teresa drives in an oversized sweater and brings an old quilt to wrap around her waist. She normally listens to Agatha Christie audiobooks, but with the tapping on the roof she loses the plot. She's driving a lawyer or banker or someone similarly suited from the Prudential to his estate in Weston. She feels like she hates him when she drops him off and sees how big his house is and that there is what looks to be a stable for horses in the back. The weak snow turns to hard rain, which splashes against and over the CR. The wheels splash through. Someone needs her down in Somerville. Okay, here goes. It is twenty minutes away and the potential passenger cancels when he sees how long it will take the CR. Someone else requests her in Dover. It's a drunk man who lives in a mansion in the woods. A drunk man who leaves a mess.

She drops the drunk off at the Wynn casino and heads to the nearest PUG. The robot arm lifts her out of the nest. Now she's cleaning up. All set. Back inside she goes. It is time, once again, to forget everything she has ever been and ever known.

22

A seagull picks at garbage in the middle of the street in Dorchester while Teresa waits for a red light to turn green. The passenger in the CR, who had his eyes glued to his phone for most of the ride, now looks apprehensively at the doors. He reaches for the window and looks out and down, seemingly to get a glimpse of the CR tires in motion. The man continues to inspect the interior nervously until she drops him off at a law office in North Quincy.

On her way to the PUG, Teresa turns on the radio and discovers the reason why the passenger had been acting strange.

A Waymo van crashed over highway guardrails yesterday afternoon in Gallup, New Mexico. The vehicle landed in the parking lot of a preschool, exploding upon impact and resulting in a fire at the school. Nine children and two teachers were killed. Eleven others are in critical condition.

Several hours pass and she does not receive a single pickup request.

On the Seer-CR app, she sees an alert:

Dear staff,

As you likely know, something awful transpired yesterday in Gallup, New Mexico. I pray for the families of the victims of this senseless accident. Our data team predicts that requests for CR vehicles will drop precipitously but please understand this will only be a temporary setback. It is not a reflection at all of the remarkable work that you do or the tremendous technology solutions we provide at AllOver. We are grateful for your service and contribution to the Holistic Apex.

Sincerely,
Verma

Teresa takes this letter as permission to go for a long walk. She exits the PUG and senses her way in the direction of the beach. Passing a corner with a Shawmut Bank and Dunkin' Donuts, she finds the shoreline and walks in the sand. It's a mild February, the sun has set, and her heavy fleece jumpsuit is enough to keep her warm.

What if the CR program shuts down due to inactivity? Here it is, her familiar worry—always proven correct—that the ground underneath her will give out eventually. She feels guilty for dwelling on it right now. Her thoughts should be with the children in Gallup and their parents, but she's felt this ache before and it's all-consuming until the inevitable happens. When things are good with work, all it means is things will get worse.

Training promised Teresa at least two beginnings. Now that she's been driving a while, all her work going forward is a journey toward an ending. How long can a middle go? She stares into the darkness beyond the beach—what is it that she even wants from this job or any—before returning to the PUG to wait for a truck driver to take her back north.

"I did nothing. I mean nothing," she says to a truck driver when she hops in his vehicle. As they drive through Quincy, she looks out the window at the signs of civilization. A Target in a strip mall complex, closed but brightly lit, and a Shell station add to the radiance of the streetlights off the interstate. "One pickup this morning. Then there wasn't a single call. I waited for hours."

"It's still new," the driver says. "They're not going to get rid of you, even if your numbers are no good, if that's what you're afraid of."

The first car she owned broke down constantly and she was always calling Triple A. Sometimes she'd have long conversations with the tow truck drivers who would give her a lift and she'd tell them all about her problems at school or with boyfriends. Some of them were good listeners, she thought, but now, almost thirty years have passed, and she doesn't remember a single one of them. This exchange, she knows, on the clock, is just as transient and one-sided.

"But the Gallup accident."

The driver shakes his head. "Stuff happens."

On the Turnpike now, out and under the Star Market overpass, Teresa wonders what it is like to shop for groceries with the highway underfoot. What would it be like to live around here? "I finally got enough saved to move out of my mother's place—"

"So, go ahead," the driver said. "Move out if you want that."

"I don't want to sign a lease and have it all crash down on me if AllOver shuts down the CR program." Out the window she sees the cloverleaf exit to Dudleyborough covered in busted wheel rubber like confetti.

"Worst comes to worst, they set you up in the call centers or fulfillment warehouses. I've seen it happen. Retention matters to them. And with this CR business, you have the upper hand. They say it's because staff are all family and neighbors, but the objective here is about keeping company secrets close."

It makes sense what the driver is saying. And thinking about it from another angle, the Waymo accident might secure her another few years—robots won't replace her anytime soon. "Hey. Do you know how I can talk to a human at AllOver?"

At a red light, he writes the number on the back of a CVS receipt. She calls and leaves a message on her bus to Brixboro out of Framingham. "I don't know who to talk to. I'm a seer, and one of the truck drivers said this is for internal AllOver support issues. I just need some help regarding a passenger incident." From the window she can see an accident on the Pike. A Nissan Pathfinder rear-ended a Buick Enclave. The drivers, both white men, look like brothers and they are arguing with each other in the breakdown lane while the passing cars slow to a crawl. The quarreling drivers look like the kind of people she'd carry in a CR.

23

On the first warm day of the year, Teresa picks up two women in Inman Square on their way to Roslindale. One of the women has a baby in a sling and when the CR reaches Jamaicaway she begins to nurse.

The other woman picks nervously at a loose thread at her sleeve. "The things I think about all day are so boring, actually," she says. "My dreams feel so predictable. There's no point in even thinking about it. Go out west. Get a classic Mustang."

The nursing woman looks up at her skeptically. "You ride horses now?"

"Oh yeah. That's a horse too, isn't it?" She laughs. "That must be how the Mustang got its name. Now if what I wanted was a horse, maybe I'd just go for it."

Two weeks have passed since the tragedy in New

Mexico and business is back to normal. After cleaning the vehicle at a PUG in Storrowton, her phone rings. "Is this Teresa? I'm so happy you called."

Teresa looks at the number on her phone. Redwood City–based. "I know it is tricky with all the phone tree systems and chatbots," says the woman calling. "And I apologize for the delay. We've got a backlog to get through. Can't hire enough. That's the drawback to being a big company. But we at AllOver always want you to feel like part of the neighborhood. Now tell me, what's your concern?"

"Wow, thanks." Teresa looks out the window at an abandoned textile mill made of crumbling bricks. "I do have a concern. And, before I begin, I should say, I know I might have misinterpreted what was happening. But I have felt this should not go unreported. I saw something happen in one of the CRs that struck me as . . . objectionable."

Objectionable. A good grown-up, professional word to voice her concerns. She was pleased to have come up with it.

"Got it," the support operator says in attentive fashion. "Hostile pax?"

"What?"

"Pax. Passengers. You got a live wire?"

Live wire. That doesn't sound quite right to her, but Teresa goes with it. "Yes, there was a man in the CR and he was grabbing for a woman who kept saying no. It went on a long time. This happened in November, but I remember it well. Gosh, four months back. I wrote down the date and time."

"So did he . . . ?"

Now she really has to be smart with her words. "I don't know the legal definitions to what I witnessed. It looked to me like sexual assault happened earlier or was about to happen. What has been eating at me is the whole time I thought something bad would happen right there in the CR while I was driving."

"Got it."

Teresa doubts herself in the space of the operator's pause. What is she reporting, after all? What's the line between Good Samaritan and nosy?

"I'm grateful for the effort you made. This was good of you to do, Teresa. And again, I apologize for the trouble it must have taken you to find our number. What you have described goes against everything that AllOver stands for as a progressively community-minded public enterprise. Send us all the information you have about the passenger. And for future reference—your trainer should have clarified this—if you ever feel unsafe or uncomfortable with pax, then end the ride. That's all you need to do. End it. There's a yellow button. That's the 'pax pause' switch—it says 'Emergency Only' next to it. You press that and pax get an alert that there's been a technical issue. We've flagged this pax as 'unsafe to pick up' temporarily. He will see, on his app, that all CRs are currently occupied whenever he tries to book again. In the meantime, we'll keep investigating."

The next morning, Teresa scrolls through Craigslist and sends messages to potential landlords, brokers, and roommates, hopeful, especially, about a listing for a basement apartment in an area of Stoughton that she doesn't know very well.

When she visits the place, an elderly woman answers the door. Teresa introduces herself as a graduate of Blue Hills Regional High Class of 1999.

"Real different now. Suppose you could say that about any place, but it's true. Only the cemeteries have gone unchanged," the woman says.

"Didn't really notice," Teresa says, unsure if she's lying or not.

Patti's son had been living in the basement, but he moved out over Christmas. He got married to a woman in Abington with a house just like this one, she tells Teresa, who signs a check for half of what she had budgeted.

"You might know my Patrick. Class of 1996. He's the youngest. Bobby and Joe were older by ten."

"I'm not sure, sorry. It was a pretty big school. I wasn't all that great at keeping in touch with even the people I used to know very well."

Patti fixes her a cup of Barry's Tea in a heavy Dorchester Pottery mug with an anchor painted on the side.

There are photos of her grown children on the mantel between Dalecarlian horses, empty candlesticks, and crystal figurines like the kind in the window display at the Christian trinket store downtown. Poppy-print wallpaper covers the wall adjacent to the avocado green stove. Lace place mats over a plastic tablecloth cover the table. The kitchen looks like it hasn't changed since Patrick—and Teresa—were kids.

"Patrick went to Amesfield. Served in Afghanistan before that. You'll see him around. Works at the Cardoso Gas on the Canton line. Oh, he wanted to be a paramedic, but it was rough on him. Still wakes up screaming some nights. Now with the new girl, things are better. Anyhow, very private down there. The foam on the walls is soundproofing."

Teresa has her own exit at the side door and a parking space if she wants it. She doesn't get a car. No furniture, but she brought the daybed down from Brixboro. No bookshelves, but boxes full of old notebooks, tax records, her brother's old sketchbook, her jewelry box with a tennis bracelet she stole from Cedars on her last day, and the one letter from her father that she never lost, from her birthday in 1988. ("You are doing very well in school. I hope you go to college.") Dinner is microwave burritos and chips and guac. Nothing to drink but tap water in coffee cups. Home at last.

She feels like the car alarm wailing inside her for years has finally been shut off.

24

The Old Jash had been a shoe factory with a view of the harbor from the section of South Boston that real estate agents renamed "Seaport" in the final year of the twentieth century. Now it's a complex of thirty-five rustic modern lofts with exposed structural beams and concrete floors. There is a heated swimming pool on the sky deck that is always empty, even in the summer. What the building doesn't have is a designated passenger pickup zone. Teresa has driven around it five times because the man who ordered the CR is late.

From the nest she can see the painted portrait of Shearjashub Edes hanging in the lobby. His stern expression mollified by a jaunty cravat in a bow, his trim Shenandoah beard emphasizes the softness of his forehead. Dr. Edes was a legendary jurist, a pediatrician, the fourteenth mayor of Boston, a reverend, and an art historian. In

1873, he published a text in three volumes, *A Treatise on the Fine Arts; or a Biographical History of the Lives and Works of Eminent Painters, Engravers, Sculptors, and Architects. From the earliest ages to the present.* That Old Jash.

Jash looks dignified, alone and unbothered in an aluminum frame. His face is the only ornament in the building's cavernous onyx lobby. Then Jash has company. The passenger makes his way out the door.

An old man in a tangerine suit. No, he's not old. He's pale with a floppy undercut and weak posture. Might be thirty-five years old or a few years younger. It isn't him, but he looks like Jord Bishop; how Jord used to look. The Jord-like presence has ordered the CR to take him five blocks to the ICA. Just five blocks. It's dark but it's nice out.

The museum is an awkward building on the water that looks like a stapler in etched glass. Tonight is an exhibition opening. A strobe light catches the CR camera eyes and Teresa looks away as she lets the man out on the curb. She notices a bouncy castle installed by the waterfront that has been painted to resemble an old Fung Wah bus. There's a long line to jump in it that the passenger snakes his way around. He is not old, but he might be the oldest person at the party. She imagines the man, as he enters the building, recognizing hundreds of people in the crowd, just as Jord, her old boss at the Brooklyn Modern, could have expected on any given night in New York City.

It is something that confuses her to this day, how

often Jord saw his classmates and not just from college. Teresa had gone to one of the largest high schools in the country, with over a thousand students in her graduating class. She never runs into former classmates in Boston, let alone New York, but Jord talked to people he knew from school and friends of the family throughout the week—classmates from as far back as kindergarten too. They grew up to be art collectors who worked on Wall Street, reporters for the *Times* who reviewed exhibitions, publishers, curators at other museums, theater directors, venture capitalists, award-wining composers, State Department undersecretaries in town for the weekend. She couldn't imagine life this densely networked, maintaining contact with others for such durations, but they were each useful to him, certainly. If Teresa had stayed in Stoughton, regardless of her brief diversion at Amesfield State just a few miles south, her life would have been provincial—tied to her past, dead-ended at the root, and defined by her context, finalizing as the dreaded Massachusetts archetype: a townie. But look at Jord, his success sprang from the flip side of what she tried to avoid: seeing old classmates from college and from high school (boarding school) every day, asking them how their mothers are doing. Jord was from New England too.

Teresa remembers the classmate she saw in the Render Falls garage. It wouldn't surprise her if some of the people she knew from school now drive Lyfts or work in Amazon warehouses.

Finding her way to the South Boston PUG, she gives the CR a deep clean. It looks fine. There was only that man going five blocks to the museum and someone at the State House on their way to Cambridge earlier, but she felt it could use an extra polish. She grabs a hose and squeegee and washes the CR inside and out. She wonders if Jord rides in CRs.

It was a bad job as soon as she met him. "Are you seeing anyone?" Jord asked, when they met for lunch, just the two of them, to discuss his vision for the department. He was three weeks into the position and this was their first time alone together. "You are what, thirty-two?" Thirty-four. "An age to get on with it, then."

The next week, Jord approached her at her desk. She reached for her notebook, expecting a new assignment; something to do with an upcoming exhibition. "Cecilia Gagnon and I were talking about you," Jord said with a grin. "Peter McCabe. You've heard of him, he's on the faculty at Bard. Well, he split with his wife last year and is out and about again. I thought, *we* thought . . ."

Teresa wanted to ask who Cecilia was, but she worried it was one of his sisters and Jord might take offense. He had all these sisters: Amelia, title proprietor of the gallery Bishop Projects on La Cienega; Charlotte, who managed corporate collections in London; Audrey, director of sculpture at Yale School of Art. Okay, maybe it was only three, but it seemed like sisters by the dozens with all the female cousins and friends too. Cecilia was a friend, it seemed like. A friend who ran a gallery.

"I haven't worked with Peter." Teresa leaned back in her chair and put away her notebook. "But he's written catalog essays in the past. Mostly mid-century stuff."

"Stuff! Well, not a bad-looking man," he said. "You could take him out for dinner, suggest we'd love another catalog essay after the redesign—"

"You want him to write for us again?"

"Sure. And I love fixing people up. I have three marriages under my belt." She looked at him blankly. He laughed again. A punchy, hooting laugh. "Not like that! You're funny. Three couples that I fixed up. I love doing this . . . stuff!"

A week later, Teresa shared hot pot with someone who seemed like he didn't want to be there either. At work, Jord asked for all the details, whispering with his hair flopping over the side of his face. She lied and said she was back with Sinisa, who she hadn't talked to, much less seen, in a year. Over drinks, she told a coworker, one of the events coordinators, about the awkward date. The coworker laughed. "Jord is pimping you out? What a weirdo." Teresa laughed with her. Yes, how strange. How funny.

And how strange and how funny that he would email her, from his office fifty feet from her cubicle, in that shaggy, incoherent fashion. She couldn't imagine he ever fired off missives like that to the board members. "Themarket eats th culture while culture producers re-plenish& provide," read one message. It was the "thesis" of a text he was writing for a literary journal edited by a friend from college. He argued, from what she could discern from it, that the art market was the perfect "vortex" of global capitalism. In what grew to several thousand sloppy words, heavy with quotes and references to Gramsci and Chantal Mouffe, he explained how freeports worked.

Teresa offered judicious feedback. "Maybe discuss what the laws are around this practice for the lay reader?" In the following email, he asked if she wouldn't mind "sprucing up" his father's Wikipedia page ("creat account login or it will shows w/th mumu ip address").

She never had strong emotions about sending or re-ceiving email before. But she found herself mentally pre-paring before opening Gmail. She felt like she did before attending a party where she wasn't sure if she'd know anyone there or not: defenseless. The worst was when she had to message Peter McCabe about invoices and poten-tial commissions. It was humiliating, like the date had been her idea and not Jord's meddling.

Sometimes Jord's garrulous fiancée would show up at the office unannounced and clomp around Teresa's desk in her cage-strap Rockstud heels and a look on her face like she was suspicious of something. The fiancée would glance at Teresa up and down and say things like, "Oh, and *you* were at the opening last night as well?" That too was embarrassing.

The department had no interns under Roz who believed such arrangement was labor exploitation, but Jord handpicked the several interns who passed through the department each season. Their names reminded her of rare flowers: Muccia, Chrysanthe, Ottiline, India, Phaedra, and Honor-Felice. Too many Serenas to count and Marinas and Francescas and Celines. Teresa couldn't tell them apart, although they worked very hard to maintain unique personalities. They all seemed to have parents or grandparents with spare apartments uptown where they stayed throughout their internships. Ottiline never showed up, but she put the Brooklyn Modern on her CV, which Teresa happened to come upon when she was googling something else. The others she would find lounging in the halls and smoking on the balcony. She never quite knew how to talk to them. Primarily she came to know them through the CVs and essays Jord sent her home with, stuffed in manila folders. He asked her to draft recommendation letters for them, that he would sign, for PhD programs and fellowships.

The interns went to different schools—Yale and Brown, most of them, others to private colleges like Wesleyan and Oberlin—but they all knew each other before their internships began. And they knew the previous interns. When they'd meet Jord for the first time, they would tell him how they knew one of his sisters or cousins: from Documenta, or a weekend at an art collector's house in coastal Connecticut, something like that. It all struck Teresa as incredibly weird. Two of the interns appeared to be secretly dating, which was cute. Teresa saw them walk into the building together, in dresses they swapped and matching Triple Canopy tote bags, rushing through the staff entrance without so much as a "hi" to acknowledge Dante, the security guard. He'd celebrated his thirtieth year at the museum the same year that Teresa began as a temp.

Teresa once complained to one of the interns about a rent increase that would make her budget tighter. "Why don't you get a part-time job?" Phaedra suggested. The girl had just come back from a ski trip in Courchevel with her parents.

Another time, the night of an opening, she found them crowded together under the vanity lights in the restroom. It was summer and the festivities spilled out into the courtyard. It was humid; the air was damp and heavy even inside where they gathered by the mirrors. Teresa felt uncomfortable in her skin, like she was covered in a layer of cellophane. The girls were gossiping about a friend who sold a memoir for a great deal of money. When Teresa arrived, they seemed almost friendly; drunk, perhaps.

"Let me do your makeup," said Muccia, who started digging in her kit.

Sure, thanks, Teresa said. She wanted to be on their

good side, not to be another grown-up who didn't appreciate the free labor they contributed.

Muccia pulled out a glass vial of foundation and burgundy lipstick encased in brass, then a sponge and a bristly brush. She mixed the foundation with dark bronzer drops and painted it on Teresa's face. Teresa tried not to wince, but it felt like the girl had spread a layer of jam over the cellophane covering her nose and chin and cheeks. Teresa left the party early and hungrily washed her face once she was home.

Then there was Clarissa. Teresa knew her as one of the interns in curatorial, the one who came to work on her first day in a black leotard, no pants, covered in a sheer white dress shirt to her knees unbuttoned in the front. She would take dramatic steps through the halls with her chin to her chest, peering up at everyone with her small darting eyes. Jord told Teresa to expect an essay from the teenager. It didn't make sense why she had been selected to contribute to an upcoming publication; in print, no less.

The essay Clarissa contributed was strange. It began with five hundred words on the "ineffable ecstasy of knowing another body intimately." There were five paragraphs of exposition before any mention of the piece, a series of abstract black-and-white photographs by Tomas Bloch that were, yes, abstractions of bodies and skin. "Bodies are the mysteries of life. Other people's bodies are another mystery. Like the taste of fresh strawberries and the soft petals of spring daffodils, the color purple and sonnets read aloud to one another late at night, we can access, in one to another, something approaching the ultimate destination in the voyage that is human life. Roberto Bolaño once wrote that 'Love must be rebuilt every morning before breakfast.' Our breakfast is eternal, an eternal unknowing, like a birdsong from a bird that is now extinct. We are constantly approaching and never knowing the ultimate truth of selfhood, both ours and others." She submitted the essay a month after the deadline.

Teresa had no idea how to approach the document apart from cutting out all but the three sentences that explained Bloch's work. Then she entered the Bolaño quote into Google. It matched with content on a website for a student paper at Brown. On the page, Teresa found the first five hundred words from Clarissa's text, published several months ago as a personal essay. As for the Bolaño quote itself, it appeared that Clarissa flubbed it. After several more searches, with and without Google Translate, Teresa stumbled upon similar lines, attributed to Gabriel García Márquez, on a spammy website called InspirationalQuotesDaily.

She sent a brief email to Clarissa: "I am sorry we won't be able to use this text, but please be in touch for other opportunities." The next morning, Jord arrived at her desk. "Audrey called. She said you told Clarissa not to contribute? Clarissa is Audrey's *mentee*." What he did not say is that her father was an executive at a corporation where Jord's sister managed collections. Connections to two Bishop sisters. At least.

"What gives you the right," Jord said. Over his shoulder, she could see the poster in his office, an illustration of a rat with the slogan "Vermine Fasciste. Action Civique." The original he had procured for the General Strike show he curated in the spring of 2016.

They were about the same height, but he stood with a threatening lean and she was still in her chair. He couldn't look at her, Jord was so upset. He glared at the ceiling and wagged his finger in front of her face. "This is extremely disruptive." Even Jord's hair was out of sorts; less Nuremberg 1937 than distressed Afghan hound, the way it matted over his eyes. "Clarissa is a once-in-a-generation talent. We need her for this publication."

Teresa pulled up the link to the student paper and showed him the essay. "It's a simple mistake, but we contracted writing that hasn't been published before—"

"This is not plagiarism. It's just the same language. Show some respect to your junior colleagues."

"The quote is misattributed." Teresa entered the lines in Google once more to justify her actions and showed him her screen. Jord mumbled something about sorting out a kill fee for the student and walked back into his office.

And a month later, she was out.

The text she had been working on about the Parallax 3, the one she told Al Jin about, she only just finished when she was called into the surprise meeting with Jord and HR. It had been the remaining pleasant part of that job: those trips to the library, scanning archives and viewing microfiche, writing into the evening and uploading her drafts to the department shared drive.

Two weeks after she cleaned out her desk, sections of that text began to appear on the museum blog. Nothing changed, no edits made, posted with no byline, only the default WordPress user name "J.B."

25

Teresa, as the CR, follows the exit from the tunnel at 16A. South Station is on the right, elegant and round, a building she rarely encounters from this angle, in its totality. Passengers are waiting for her in the Leather District across the green space from Chinatown Gate. It is early morning and everyone is walking with coffee. An old man walks out with flowers. How sweet. He enters a parked car with a woman in the passenger seat. It could be his wife. He puts the flowers in the back seat. Maybe those flowers were for a friend. Maybe someone died. Maybe it's his sister and the flowers are for his wife. Maybe it's his wife and the flowers are for his sister. Maybe it's his sister and their mother died. Teresa drives away and wonders for the next twenty minutes whether a stranger has died and the people in the other car are in grief. Later in her shift, she waits for a funeral procession to pass, and this stranger's confirmed death strikes her as an inconvenience.

On her way home, she picks up blackout curtains, duct tape, a cookbook, and a pot. She mounts the curtains like a Band-Aid over her slim basement windows. There's an old lamp by her bed that Patrick left, and the light in the bathroom is bright enough to illuminate the whole space. It doesn't feel strenuous, when she's up in that nest, but when she gathers her laundry to wash, her tank tops and leggings smell sharp like a grapefruit left in the sun. She returns to the store for a foam roller, lightbulbs, and another brand of laundry detergent.

Her schedule sounds normal upside down. She wakes up at five o'clock. She is out at seven and home by nine. Five in the afternoon, seven at night, and nine after sunrise. Her first passengers are on their way home after work. Her final passengers are at the start of a brand-new day while hers is ending. Sometimes, when there's a pickup in the North End, she wonders if she will see any of the people who were standing outside Al Jin's brother's window. Everyone who rides the CR in the morning—her evening—radiates that kind of hope, that morning hope, as she remembers. She wishes she could bottle it and take it home with her; to reapply that hope when she wakes, late in the afternoon. No one wakes up at that hour with that brightness.

• • •

After the Brooklyn Modern, there was a year of chasing leads, applying for jobs—applying for *museum jobs*, which tended to call for a background and skill set that Teresa never officially acquired. Still, she had felt hopeful because there are art museums everywhere. The posts in cities, where, say, the international art crowd with their asymmetrical bobs and Ivy League or equivalent educations might be less inclined to hang a hat, where it's harder to make a scene and find a date, well, those cities were good enough for Teresa, who began arduous application processes with institutions in and near Savannah, Tampa, Burlington, Columbus, Overland Park, Port Townsend, Tuscaloosa, and Abilene. All the while, Teresa existed on another plane, in an airport terminal in her mind, all the gates lined up with this set of destinations: Savannah, Tampa, Burlington, Columbus, Overland Park, Port Townsend, Tuscaloosa, Abilene. Each location a different future, but a destination is always the future. A future was all she needed. When would she board and where would she land? Until she knew, she was suspended before the jetway.

Through this period, which had felt interminable until it stopped, Teresa learned to hide the sense that she was slipping away. It felt like red paint dripping inside her. She did not fight any of it, did not complain about any of it. It was a good job and "too small for her," her friends said; she could do better, she will do better. At birthday parties, trips to the beach, and barbecues on the

Fourth of July, sometimes the red paint spilled out. She would break into tears spontaneously when she spoke about something, anything, with a hint of solemnity—a poem she read on the internet written by a soldier who died in Iraq—that was all she needed and she was dripping red again. Dripping all over her unsuspecting friends. The tears bubbled out and gushed; she would ask to excuse herself—she had to; allergies, she said. Her hair fell out in clumps. It was nothing. Something better was on the horizon. Had to be. Until there wasn't. There were a half dozen interviews over the phone and over Skype, and a half dozen institutions went with someone else.

She'd pick up *Art in the World* at the library and see Muccia's and India's bylines. Listed in the *ArtPractice* masthead, there's Phaedra, now a contributing writer, writing capsule reviews and profiling the latest Turner Prize recipient. Muccia interviewed Honor-Felice about an exhibition she curated at the Whitney. She named the people who got her to where she is today, including "Jord Bishop. One of the good ones and fully supportive of his staff at the Brooklyn Modern. A mentor and a friend, really." Ottiline, who never showed up, was named assistant curator at the Brooklyn Modern four years after her alleged internship. Chrysanthe switched careers and became head of marketing at the internet retailer Felicity Lake, which sells bamboo-based hair elastics it calls "rounds" and barrettes, which the website inexplicably refers to as "put-togethers." On an arts job board, Teresa noticed a listing for a "catalog and digital editions editor" at Bishop Projects. Six months later, Clarissa's name appeared as the sender of the gallery's newsletter. In Clarissa's introductory note, she said it was a thrill to move to Los Angeles and an honor to work with her mentor, Amelia Bishop.

One of the Celines got famous for a shitposting Twitter account. Tweets like "h8 it here lol" next to a photo of something random like the greeting card aisle at Walgreens. All of this was later packaged as a book, *Broke(n) Millennial*, which could be found for sale in the front tables at Urban Outfitters for most of 2016. In the acknowledgments section, Celine thanks Jord, two Bishop sisters, and several former Brooklyn Museum interns. Of a dozen other people, including her literary agent, she effused, "You believed in me when no one else did and you've been my favorite people in the world since we were all just scrappy kids surviving on Top Ramen." Celine had gone to Harvard. And Brearley.

Teresa's friends sent her links to job listings they found on LinkedIn or Indeed. They tried to convince her that her skills matched the requirements even when she knew they didn't. She couldn't afford her studio anymore, but they had her over for housesitting or watching the cat. There was always a couch or spare bedroom to sleep in the meantime for a week or a weekend. Sometimes a hostel for a couple nights at a time. Just getting back on her feet. She was in a constant state of learning where someone keeps their silverware, whether or not they have a microwave and how to turn on their shower knob; always in the state of arriving at a new place, while perpetually reminded it was a settled-in home that was not her home. If it were a Hollywood movie, she would have snooped through their things, tried on their clothes; isn't there always a scene where the houseguest secretly dresses up in the hostess's most expensive gowns? But Teresa wanted the very opposite; she looked for the rooms with the least furnishings. At one friend's apartment, she set a pillow down in the hallway by the front door and slept there, because it was painted white and free of ornament. It was the only place in the apartment where she didn't have to contend with his taste, his mind, his preferences as expressed in the salon hang art on every wall and ginger-colored throw rugs. She was grateful for the generosity of her friends, but the very matter of this exchange was a reminder of her unsettled ground. A couple she knew went to Moscow for two months and let her stay, ostensibly to water their plants while they were gone. Their house was huge for New York but modest, so normal for anywhere else, and furnished with IKEA mixed with solid wood heirlooms. She wondered what kind of salaries her friends made to afford such a place, but they lived so normally. They were not fancy and careless, but they made it work from an unfamiliar stratosphere, with an unfamiliar perspective on what counts as normal and thrifty. Because they were normal. And they were thrifty. That first week funneled into the second and third weeks. Five weeks became seven. She had a week left to figure out where to go next. Résumés went out each day, some interviews were booked, but nothing moved beyond that. The economy was good. The problem had to be her. "You were too good for that job," her now-dwindling group of friends continued to say. She began to notice the universities listed on their own LinkedIn pages. Failing to cinch a future, she was trapped in a world of departures without learning her gate or boarding time. Perhaps she missed her flight and didn't know it. She couldn't make a home for herself in the terminal.

A year had gone like this, occupying other people's apartments left empty while the resident went someplace for a fellowship or summer in the Hamptons. It was strange how this crowd shared their property casually. The thought occurred to her, their generosity might never have been extended this way, if any of them had seen the micro-studio where she used to live. Living "between places" meant something very different to them.

"You write, don't you?" said an American heiress in town from Berlin only minutes after they met. "I have a cottage in the South of France. I love having writers and artists stay. They fill the place with a creative energy." Teresa considered it but bristled at the fees to apply for a passport.

There were reasons to complain. Internally. She never begrudged anything aloud, but certain extensions of kindness come with cryptic humiliations. A note on the counter would say "eat anything you like." All the produce in the fridge was rotted. Some left old, mildewy sponges by the sink that couldn't possibly make a dish clean. She never thought of herself as a neat freak, but inside another person's home, she could see what chores other people left for last or never. Unknown hairs on the shower curtain. The crumbs and crust collecting on a rack that was to be used to set clean dishes. She told herself not to be fussy. Sure, she was lazy about things, and sometimes she was gross, but she was living with other people's grossness and not her own. Teresa was tired of thanking people, always expressing gratitude—she felt it, but it was exhausting. She would have much preferred to be generous with her friends than the one benefiting from their generosity. If nothing was owed, she could forget the exchange, all guileless and guiltless rather than forever chained to and defined by it.

Two days before her friends returned from Moscow, she decided on a plan. Or the plan fell on her. She sold what she could from her storage unit and donated or threw the rest away. She spent three months on an old cot in the den of her old house in Stoughton. Her father said he was happy to see her and she could stay as long as she wanted. She sent her résumé to every staffing agency from Canton to Manchester-by-the-Sea. Walked to the commuter rail every morning for her assignments at the front desks and cubicles in endless interchangeable downtown corporate offices. Just getting back on her feet. Sometimes she would ride the Chinatown bus to New York on weekends and stay on couches and in guest rooms belonging to her waning list of friends. No one ever said anything, but she felt their frustration with her. The plan had been to save enough money to return, but in the course of scrounging up money, she had become a tourist, a visitor. She emailed and initiated these emails and told everyone she was still looking without mentioning her whereabouts (a dusky cubicle at the Old Mill Container Corporation with stacks of earnings reports printed for her to enter into a spreadsheet). It was a protracted ending. There were weddings she wasn't invited to; some had babies that were toddlers before long. There were divorces too, but no one died, as far as she could tell from her Facebook feed. There were lives lived and routines formed and new cliques. She stopped initiating emails. What else was there to say? It was too depressing to explain why it had been three years or five or seven. These, she finally understood, had been the feet that she was meant to get back on.

What followed were months gliding through windowless and dusty Airbnb shares in Boston, reserved and paid for on her credit card. She would stay in these locations for five days, sometimes ten. The dates would correspond with various short-term gigs in telemarketing and at front desks. Every time was the same drill: retrieving keys from a lockbox on a gate, a list of instructions from the phantom roommate with the Wi-Fi password and a list of places nearby with good tacos or flat whites. The posters on the walls were different, some beds were firmer, and others more or less toasty. There were rooms with sputtering heaters that kept her up all night, sometimes it was commotion from a couple arguing in the apartment one door over. Photographs and mementos on the walls often revealed the story why this person or that was not there, while Teresa slept in their beds. One guy had the word "TULUM!" in all caps and a line marking dates on his calendar that corresponded exactly with the dates that he was gone and she was there. Stepping inside all these apartments, all these homes belonging to someone else, she grew overwhelmed by the orders and structures that made sense to them; like why some people buy hundreds and hundreds of different bottles of shampoo and leave them all out in the shower. These were rooms in shared apartments and the roommates were ciphers she might spot in passing on the way to brush her teeth in the bathroom down the hall. She never remembered any of them, and conversations, if they happened, were always tense and brief.

Another week at a place in the South End. A child on a tricycle pedaled in first. "Is she the new guest, Mommy?" A sparse one-bedroom, BU grad student housing according to the signage, with the mother's textbooks in a pile next to a small box of toys. The mother and daughter slept on an air mattress in the living room behind a curtain. She could hear them talking quietly in the kitchen sometimes, switching back and forth from English to Mandarin. Teresa had the sense she was witnessing a moment the girl would one day remember and cherish— that things had been hard but somehow her mother made it work. And Teresa herself would fold inside a spectral blur of guests in the girl's memory of this time. She wouldn't be remembered at all. The way it should be.

But now with the CR, finally, Teresa has a role and place. She has somewhere to go once she drops off this man from his office in Seaport to his house in Jamaica Plain. There is a circle of menacing turkeys strutting outside the PUG. They scurry away as the doors open up to receive the driverless vehicle. When she cleans the CR out, she finds that the passenger had left a plastic package of oyster crackers under the seat. It is crushed to crumbs. She tips her chin back and swallows the contents like a baby bird as it receives a treat.

26

The Impreza is out in the driveway covered in a yellow veil of pollen. Parked behind it is a rental car with the last of Teresa's belongings packed in the trunk. There isn't much. Her mother sits on the front porch. She has said nothing at all today, not even when Teresa dropped three heavy paper bags of CVS prescriptions on the kitchen counter with a thud.

Teresa turns on the ignition, but before she reverses out, her mother walks over to the window of the car, her face expressionless. "When I pass, Teresa, everything you need is in those boxes in the shed." Driving home, to her home, she remembers how, when she first moved to Brixboro, her mother would stay up late watching television until two in the morning. Teresa couldn't sleep until the daybed became a bed. She had to wait for scraps of privacy.

All proof of her life is in papers and files stuffed in

shoe boxes and boot boxes, some sturdier than others with duct tape to keep the corners square. She opens one of the boxes and finds a journal she kept for six months in 2018, including nine elliptic entries. Flipping through the pages, her past self opaque to her present self, she stops on a page written clearly. It says, "I don't like to be treated like I am made of years. Years don't indefinitely replenish themselves over. And even if years were renewable or unlimited, I would still suffer the absence of time that is in waiting. I have lost years waiting, years where nothing happened. I paid in time that I can never get back. Time I never chose to spend this way. If the years were layaway, then I could redeem this time. Now as I look at what I have written on this page I see that my capital Y looks like a T. I guess I don't like being treated like I'm made of tears also. 8/14/2018." What happened that day? She doesn't know and the notebook doesn't say. Could have been an unpleasant Airbnb or a regrettable Tinder date, both of which she'd had too many of that year to recall with any clarity. She decides to throw out the journal but the basket beside the stove feels too lightweight for the task. Teresa walks outside toward the barrels in the driveway that Patrick takes out on Sunday nights.

Patti opens her front door and waves as Teresa rips up the notebook and throws it in with the jagged delivery package fins in the recycling bin. "I made lasagna. Come have some, Teresa!"

The second hand ticks loud on Patti's clock with illustrations of different types of birds—cardinal, blue bird, chickadee—circling around the hours. The old woman hands her a warm plate with a perfect square of wavy pasta layers heavy on the cheese and slices of zucchini from the garden. Semitrucks pass outside the open windows against the buzz of moths flying up to the mesh screens and fluttering away. They take their plates to the TV room. Falconer Guidry is being profiled in the news hour report.

Teresa always assumed that Falconer had exaggerated his life story until she saw the camera pan over the manufactured home in rural Arkansas where he had grown up. The news correspondent accompanying him looks over the house with its weak porch and runs in the window screen, the orange siding and thick concrete base. "What are you thinking now? This used to be your home."

"This is intense. I must admit, I wasn't prepared," Falconer says with a sigh. "When you live close to the dirt, you learn what matters, fast. And what you can't live without." The camera follows him on a tour of his old elementary school. Falconer is investing millions in the region, building computer labs and coding schools with scholarships available to all the students. "Improbable as it sounds, it's hard to give my money away. Not the way you think," he says, in another moment of introspection. "I'd give it all away, but that's not possible under capitalism. I don't always know how a charity is run or whether the funding will be extracted to its full potential. There is a long process of research, on my part, before I cut a check—and, of course, the preferable course of action is that an effective government works for the people and taxes billionaires such as myself equitably. Until then, what I do know, what I am an expert in, is this town. That's why I'm giving back."

The two men ride a CR around town. "The simplest case for driverless cars is that only technology can be trusted to always follow speed limits and precautions," Falconer says. "Human nature is to race through thickly settled districts at all hours no matter how many 'children playing' signs you put up." Teresa contemplates this. She does follow rules. If she were to tip above the speed limit a deafening alarm would wail through the nest and encourage her to stop. "Humans can't be programmed— we have spirits. That spirit is the beauty of humanity, but it's also what makes us monsters on the road. Machines live by rules. Machines don't experience road rage. Machines are calm any hour of the day, in any driving conditions. There's nothing safer than what we are sitting in. But ultimately, I built the CR to be the very last vehicles on the road. Automobile technology has ravaged our cities and our climate. We need sensible human-centric solutions to intractable problems like highway blight and carbon emissions."

The segment cuts to show the news correspondent

facing Falconer in a corporate reception area. The correspondent has a wry look and holds a notebook that he
doesn't write in or look at. "You have your share of critics,"
he says. "The protests outside the Norcross warehouses."

"The socialists, the neo-Luddites who believe they
are carrying on in the tradition of Ned Ludd and smash-
ing the looms and messing up the textile mills of today,"
Falconer answers with a dismissive laugh. "What are
they building? What kind of tomorrow will their rhetoric
bring? A world in which only Harvard elites get to be
heard, get to be free? Socialism as an ideology is uniquely
attractive to the wealthy because it validates their lifestyle. When you get to be like me, very rich, you live in an
isolated world that sounds a lot like communism. People
do favors for you. Every day, I'm sent food, clothing, gad-
gets, presents. Gifts in exchange for my attention, my
goodwill. When I needed these things, when I was down,
where were they? It's simple: I wasn't considered elite,
therefore I wasn't deemed worthy of elite-communism."

What he's saying reminds Teresa of her old art world
friends. The way they let her use their houses because
they couldn't conceive that she wasn't rich like them.

"Everyone who has attended Harvard has experienced some version of communism. And it comes at the
expense of others. But at the very bottom of the economic ladder, you see true connections. Families come
first. That's how I was raised. When I have one shirt, I
give you my shirt, because you need it more than me.

With AllOver, I instill these values, my belief in anti-capitalist public goods through the private sector, to build a more just and collaborative society."

Teresa looks up from her empty plate and her land-lady shuts the TV off.

"What do you think of the CR?" Patti asks.

"Too expensive for me."

"I'd get claustrophobic. But I can see why he did it," Patti says. "A car is as American as America gets. He's striking right at the heart of American culture. Road trips, Ford assembly lines, Route 66. You get your name in the middle of that history and you make a legacy."

Teresa looks at Patti. "Do you believe him? The things he said. Do you think he was sincere?"

Patti laughs loudly. "Of course it's bullshit. But what can you do? Bullshit that sounds right is better than bullshit that sounds wrong." Teresa listens to the cars pass outside and wishes she shared Patti's skepticism.

At South Station, an Amtrak to New York has been delayed. The station platforms are alight with exasperated crowds. It is crowded everywhere, with people dressed in nice clothes inspecting the menus at the restaurants in the food court. She finds her way between a suited elbow and the coat of another and finds a quiet place to wait inside Jimmy's Newsstand. The display tower for *Holistic Apex: Solving the Future with Human Solidarity and Collaborative*

Tomorrow-Building is gone, but she finds a stack of five copies on a table in the back affixed with half-off stickers. She purchases a copy. Why not.

Two minutes until the commuter rail will depart, Teresa dashes for the first car with thirty seconds to spare. She stands by the door window and at the third stop, an old-timey billboard for a diner catches her eye. It's at an angle that she can only see from this spot in this train car, and despite forty years of riding this line she has never seen it before.

> 24 hours. Around The Clock. Anything You
> Want. If It Is Open Tomorrow, It Is Open
> Yesterday and Today. Any 24, We've got
> an open door.

Teresa counts the numbers on the illustrated clock quietly to herself: 1, 2, 3 . . . to 12. Then she reaches for her new book.

"I had always wanted so badly to believe in meritocracy," Falconer writes in the introduction. "I wanted to believe that if I only worked harder, good things would come my way, because then I'd be in control. True control comes from collaboration. We cannot fulfill human purposes in isolation. That's why I built my company, AllOver. These values inform every moment of my life, and every decision I make I think of in terms of potential outcomes for the global community. In these pages, I will show you how to fight your inner judge and jury; together we will combat modern addiction to our personal suffering. Separate we are small. As a progressive society, we flourish as the Holistic Apex."

She puts the book back in her bag. It's hard to focus on it. She feels, all the time now, like she did on those nights out in New York with dozens of people, conversations on either side of her that she'd slip in and out of and finally entirely out of; sitting quietly in the middle of a table because on neither side was a way in.

Ever since she's been driving the CR, her brain has been spinning dizzy like tumbling sheets in a washing machine.

t's grad season and the traffic is heavy with U-Hauls, four-door sedans with each seat taken. Cars with out-of-state plates, some from as far away as California. The rain is falling hard and everything looks like a movie in black and white between thunder and flashes except for the red brake lights and kelly green highway signs overhead. Teresa blinks when she exits the dark city into the bright yellow tunnel. Through this maze of concrete walls and bridges, over wet streets slick with glitter in the chilly downpour, she moves along as the digital map tells her, pounding out the mental map of Boston that she has accumulated, of all the boa constrictors and roller-coaster tracks of highway, in and out and around the city.

At the end of a whirling shift—five sets of passengers and no more than a forty-minute break between any of them—Teresa finds her way to the nearest PUG. It is located bayside in the Squantum marshland. The path to it is made of gravel and crushed clamshells that crunch under the CR tires. Crying seagulls fly overhead. Beyond the PUG, in the water, are remnants of a bridge that was demolished twenty years before. The sturdiness of the abutments, missing a connecting structure, suggests an invisible bridge that only an invisible man in an invisible automobile could travel over. That island had been a homeless shelter and drug treatment facility. Abandoned in ruin and with no road access, it is an invisible clinic for the invisible in need because of invisible boundaries in a confusing state of ownership: the island is Boston, what had been the bridge is part of Quincy.

The PUG yawns open to receive the vehicle and Teresa notices another CR inside. The two driverless cars together remind her of the blueberry branches of vehicles inside Render Falls. Once the doors close, the robot arm carries her to the ground. She shakes her ankles and wiggles her fingers and wrists and remembers what her body feels like once again without its exoskeleton.

She steps cautiously over the tangled multicolored cables that are looped from the gold robot. Teresa cleans the vehicle swiftly and returns the supplies to the custodial closet where she finds Al Jin, resting silent and peaceful on the floor.

Al has his back pressed against the curve of the

PUG's inner wheel well. He raises his arms above his head. "Oh, hey. I was just stretching," he says, looking up at her.

Without thinking she lies down next to him. While ordinarily she might ask someone how they are and what's new, she realizes she has no answer to this question herself. All previous twelve hours are compressed into underdeveloped snapshots: her memory of the backs of the passengers' heads and the way the rain made the city lights look like strung-up tennis bracelet diamonds. It doesn't matter what she says or doesn't say. He begins talking real fast about how much he misses taking his bike out. "I'm a liar," he says, holding out one finger and crossing it with the other. "And a thief. I cannot be trusted. That's three," he says, counting on his fingers with each item. "I'm forgetful, fickle." He continues to count. She burrows her head into his shoulder. It seems like a good place to fall asleep.

"But right now," she says, "you're just lying here with me. Where'd you come from?"

"Airport pickups have been my thing," he says. "I like the idea of helping people get out of the city. But then I get stuck bringing people back to the city too."

He screams with laughter for no reason. Then he whispers, "The craziest thing is I think that someday I will walk into the past and see it all unfold exactly as it happened." She doesn't know how to respond to what he said. He keeps talking anyway. "Not even my past. Anyone's past. I really do think this. I will walk around some corner and find my way to 1972 or 1986 or another time. Some old bar that doesn't exist anymore. Everyone's got bushy baseball card mustaches and plaid shirts and old blue jeans. Eddie Money on the jukebox."

"But then you are outside it." The pain in her shoulders has shot down to her lower back. She presses her back against the wheel well and relaxes somewhat.

"I guess."

She'd like to look in his eyes but he's staring at the ceiling. "Or do you imagine yourself inside? Talking to people?"

"No, I imagine myself standing there. Like the ghost of Christmas present or past. Like any kind of ghost." He's laughing again. "Look, I honestly believe that at any moment there's a nonzero chance that I will observe 1997 or 1962 or whatever time that isn't this one unfolding in front of me. I will only get a moment with it, but it will be completely real."

"Where would it happen?"

"Anywhere. I'll step on the train at Coolidge Corner and think everything is normal. Then I see I'm behind two guys in, like, power tweed suits discussing the best model of cordless phone from Service Merchandise."

"And then when you get off the train, things will go back to normal?"

He thinks for a moment before responding. "I don't know yet."

"Sounds intense."

"I think I hold on to memories in an intense way. And I connect to the past in an intense way," Al says. He sounds calm as he explains, "Sometimes I feel it in supermarkets. Old ones. Most supermarkets are all revamped inside with organics sections and specialty aisles. But there's an old Shaw's by my brother's house and I went there on Christmas Eve one time by myself. He told me to get some milk because they needed milk. I looked down at the floor. It has this old tile pattern with hexagon shapes in maroon and gray and orange. I really thought it was happening. I thought if I turned around, I'd find out that this is Christmas Eve in 1986 and all these people are on their way to see their families. The women have big permed-out hair and their little kids sit in the shopping carts. Everyone in Velcro monochrome Reebok high-tops. This scenario came to me all clear in my mind. I imagined that there'd be a guy behind me in a tan corduroy jacket, shitty haircut, nerd glasses, the works. He's divorced and the wife has the kids over the holiday but he's got this new girlfriend. He's shopping for all these items to make a Christmas meal for the first time with the girlfriend. And putting all this shit in his cart he doesn't need because he wants to impress her. Like, the real butter, not margarine this time, all for this woman. He'll probably fuck up the cooking and they'll get takeout in the end. But he's going to have a really good Christmas in 1986, that man, whoever he is, and right now he's so excited. He'll remember Christmas but he'll forget all about the grocery shopping. As soon as I thought of him, I felt so sure it was happening. I looked at the quarts of milk and I looked at the floor and I thought, okay, great, it's transition time. I don't know why. Maybe what threw me off is that milk bottle packaging hasn't changed so much. I guess they don't do pictures of missing kids anymore, but a quart is still a quart, you know? And people don't really look at their phones in grocery stores. You can't really push a cart and text message and on Christmas Eve, especially, you have to make a beeline for whatever is on your shopping list. Anyway, it didn't happen. It stayed Christmas Eve 2019."

Teresa leans back over the wheel well and closes her eyes. "And the girlfriend. What's she like?"

"I wouldn't have seen her. Just the guy but I didn't see the guy this time either. It just came to me. Look, I know it sounds crazy, but these are real people. They're real lives that happened. Could still be alive."

"Will you ever see Cedars again?"

"Cedars?"

"The department store. I worked there in high school."

"Oh, that Cedars. That's where I had to go for a vaccination. What was left of the old place on the second floor of the CambridgeSide Galleria. At least I think it was—could have been an old Caldor. No, Cedars sounds right. That was it."

Teresa opens her eyes and turns to look at him. He

rubs his forehead into her ear. She's still not sure what to make of anything he has said.

"I remember I could see what had to be the family portrait studio with oversized crayon pieces and alphabet blocks that kids could sit on. But I don't remember much. I just wanted to get it over with. They had us stand beside a section in the middle with empty glass cases."

"Oh, the vitrines." Teresa imagines what the skeleton of Cedars must look like from the inside. All the inventory gone, the vitrines like empty fish tanks; but of the portrait studio, she might see carpeted booster seats lying around and the fake oil-painted canvas screens. The Cambridge store might have been arranged differently than the Stoughton location, but the glass brick and checkerboard floors would have been the same. The lights down would have reminded her of the path she used to take through the display cases full of paint color swatches. Maybe she would have seen what had been a jewelry counter and wonder if she got it wrong and it had actually been the place for cosmetics. She wishes there had been a secret Facebook group back when she worked there, for all the sales associates who worked in the department, all over the country, to hang out and joke about their random encounters with strange customers. They'd share their feelings about the tennis bracelets and engagement rings. Honest appraisals only.

"That must have been a nice place to work," Al says.

"I'd love to go but I can't conjure up specific places. It just has to happen."

"Do you ever feel it about your own memories?"

"Not really. If I walk past a place I used to live, I'll remember things. Everyone does, I think. But I can't go back to where I was at that time. It's other people's lives that I feel this way about. Strangers. I probably shouldn't be telling you this. I really trust you is what I'm saying. I don't share this kind of stuff, normally."

"Can you go different places from here, Al? Do you think you could turn around Mass Ave and see Hemingway in Paris or Rita Hayworth at the Hollywood Canteen?"

"No, I'd be tied to the physical location. Only the time changes. And my sense is when it finally occurs it will be something basic. People in an ordinary place. Like some bowling alley from 1987 that's now a Whole Foods. I will remember what they will forget."

Teresa catches a blast of a bowling alley memory from 1987. She feels it in hazy fragments. The shoes, red and blue, split and so old they could have housed a hundred years of feet. The malted milk and cheese smell of the insoles and the squeak when the heels skid on the shiny synthetic wood lanes. It was a place that was always partially obscured with cigarette smoke and fragmented light from a cheap mirror ball overhead. The candlepins and grapefruit-size bowling balls in swirling maroon and marbleized forest green. The balls were tiny but always seemed to weigh as much as she did—maybe they did the last time she played. He's right. The bowling alley that she remembers has to be a Whole Foods now.

"You really think you will travel through time?"

He nods.

She's laughing but she believes him. Well, she believes he believes this. "So you are like the chosen one."

He shakes his head and folds his arms. "It's not like that. No, no."

"Does that mean anyone can? Could I?"

"No, it's just me, but I'm not special because of it." He gets up from the wheel well, stretches his arms again, and looks at his feet. "I mean, it hasn't happened to me yet, but I know it is going to happen to me."

The ocean sounds wicked at night and she can hear the rain above it. Pouring. Storming. "That's lonely." She meant to say, "That's lovely." But the wrong word came out. Or the right one.

"How was your ride?" she asks.

"It was okay."

When she was younger, she would go to warehouse parties in way-off places, Foxboro or farther away. Riding in the back of someone's father's pickup truck, already too high to remember how she got there, and leaving in blacked-out disarray. There would be nothing for miles, not even trees, just dead pine needles, straw, and junked cars. They'd park in fields so quiet she could hear the straw crunch under her shoes above the dirt supporting her weight at every step. At the entrance to the warehouse the silence and black blanket of sky thick with stars would give way to annihilating noise and lasers and smoke machines. That was four, five years of her life. In the years before she moved closer to Boston and merged into its upper-echelon nightlife with cocktail lounges and nightclubs where the DJs carried business cards and got paid. She didn't like the music, but she loved the sense that to go there, and to be part of it, was like a consensual surgical removal of her time and memories. Days and nights were lost in her mind like she never lived them. She got good grades, she did what she had to do, but on the weekends, she could lose herself entirely at these parties. It was like being in the center of a tornado, thrown to another by chance, awakening in someone's arms, in the middle of a near-empty dance floor with someone in her face. The moments of initiation were the first to fade from memory. How it started was unclear. She never knew who they were, just that it happened, which she could scarcely recall the next day. They would leave the party in another car or truck. These people seemed like apparitions that she herself made up to make her life seem more interesting to her.

Now she's out with Al in the salty wetlands where it drizzles. Running in circles and screaming through the cordgrass and cattails while getting wet. Teresa ducks under the sparkling rock PUG and he follows. How did she end up at warehouse parties in Foxboro? There was a vehicle and it took her there. What else was there to do but get inside and ride? How is she, right now, underneath a PUG with Al, cleaving room for them in the sticky earth, one hand on her head to protect it from rubbing against the cinder blocks at the base of the structure? Her right knuckle raw and bloody as it rubs against the cinder blocks. What else is there to do but get inside and ride? It is dark and endless down there. An image flashes through her mind of a mudslide in the rain. The PUG will slip and trap them both underneath, like the inside of a locket, before crushing and suffocating them whole, the end of that.

It doesn't happen.

They emerge from the lair where the rain has mellowed into fog. The night sky is loosening with the impending day.

"This is the only thing I like about the job," he says, calling in for a truck lift, when they return to the PUG. "Hitchhiking. It's like a dream from a generation that's not mine. Did I tell you about the time I tried to rent the house where Kerouac was born? I thought about it but I didn't know what to do with myself up in Lowell." The truck arrives and they hop in. They are muddy like teenagers who just got caught. Teresa sits in the middle. Her leggings are on backward, she realizes. She forgot her quilt in the CR, but she's got her license in the travel wallet under her shirt, strapped around her waist. She's going home.

28

Nasty out," the truck driver says.

"Sure is," Al says.

Classic rock on the radio plays loudly and they are whipping past the Neponset River. Tall brick buildings on either side stretch out before the dawn. There's the old cidery and old mills with domino-shaped windows. It is an office park now. Teresa had a temp job on the sixth floor of that mill. She would look out the window at the canal while she directed callers to various extensions, pressing buttons and speaking into a headset. The windows faced east, and in the morning, at a time of day just like now, she had to avert her eyes and swivel her mesh-back chair to face the brick wall to hide from the light.

"It's not so bad," Al says to the driver. "You think about, like, Henry Ford factory workers. Backbreaking labor but you got paid enough to own a house, raise a family. It's like that. They pay us and give us time so I can't complain. This isn't Lyft, where you'd feel broke and cheated all the time."

"I'll say," the driver says. "And I do appreciate the technology. The self-driving doesn't work at all like they tell everyone but on some of the empty roads I can eat chips and keep my hands off the steering wheel."

Al tries to talk with the driver about the Celtics but they can barely hear each other over the music. He is easygoing about it; they both are. "Have you got a cat back there?" Al says, joking. "I hear something." The driver remains quiet and focuses on the road.

"Okay, I just heard mewing. For real," Al says loudly. "That is definitely mewing."

Teresa hears it too. Low, catlike. Something inside the truck. Something is broken.

"Wait." Al sits still and looks forward at the road ahead. "You do have a cat! That is a cat, man."

"Look, I can explain." The driver turns off the radio. The cat has also gone silent. Then it mews again loudly.

"We won't tell anyone." Al turns to look behind their seats. He reaches out toward the sleeper birth and taps a crate covered in fleece blankets. "Can we see her?"

"Sure, you can see her," the driver says, as Al unhooks the crate to release the driver's secret companion. An old tabby cat hops in the space between them. Al gently carries her to his lap. Teresa scratches the cat's heavy hind legs. Lady Moose. She likes to doze on the dash and play in the passenger footwell. "My sister's cat," the driver says. "She's been in the hospital awhile."

"Wonder if I could get a passenger cat to keep me company. Guess the nest is not a great place for an animal," Al says. "Maybe I could switch to trucks. Whaddya think, dude? Have I got what it takes?" He looks into the cat's eyes as he pets her. "What have I been doing with myself? When all this time I could have been truck-driving with a cat beside me."

The driver tells them what it used to be like before AllOver. This tight schedule is just about impossible. He sleeps in his truck, fucked up with child support, and lost his health insurance because he doesn't even know what state he counts as a resident in. "The place in Nevada where I got evicted? My sister's in Florida, where I don't know anyone else? And this cat, I don't know why they'd care but I know they'd give me problems if they found out. When I first started driving, it was the nineties. Analog. No one cared. Could have a baby hippo with me. So long as it poops outside and I get my job done, it don't matter." The driver keeps his eyes on the road. "But that's the way it is. No going back."

Teresa looks at the knobs and metering devices on the driver's dashboard. It's a complicated setup, like a cockpit, like the nest.

"You know what I actually think of AllOver?" Al

says. "It's a mafia. They get a cut of everybody's business. Every transaction, they're in the middle. Protection racketeering economics. Cosa Nostra shit."

Teresa is startled by his blunt assessment of their employer. "What if they hear you?"

He frowns and nods back at the cat crate. "What? You think they got a seer stuffed back there?"

His place is closer and he will be dropped off first. "Want to stay with me?" he asks Teresa quietly. She could. "Text me," he says. "Anytime."

"I will." She says this unconvincingly and looks down at the tag of her inside-out backward leggings.

"You keep Lady Moose out of trouble!" Al shouts to Tom when his feet are on the ground.

Teresa pulls the sun visor down and glances at herself in the vanity. There are streaks of dirt on her cheek running into her hair. The mud has dried, and it shakes off in clumps. She licks her fingers and cleans the rest of it off like a cat. She thinks about Al and how happy he was with Moose. She thinks about his brother's apartment again. That was a good night.

In the light of day she returns to her basement apartment. The duct tape at one corner of the window is loose but the curtain hasn't fallen yet. There's blood at her knuckles from the cinder blocks. She bandages them. On the counter is the cookbook, open on a recipe for beet galettes. Teresa is too wound up to sleep and instead peels carrots. She's teaching herself to cook. The water boiling sounds like company in the empty apartment. The sound makes the basement feel less lonely.

Al is three years older. The same age, basically. But if they had met when she was eighteen and he twenty-one, it would have felt like he'd been free and out living in the world for three years; that he'd lived a whole lifetime in those three years. When does that feeling change?

The water boiling reminds her of the time she and Sinisa printed directions off the internet on how to steam a lobster. He had never had lobster before. They went to the supermarket together and stared at the weird buggy creatures crawling over one another in the tank, those bright bands on their claws like clipped wings. She and Sinisa looked at each other. Did they want to carry a crustacean home, squirming in the box, like a helpless new pet? "I'm not hungry now," Sinisa said. They turned around and got a pizza.

Teresa had never boiled water alone until this year and sometimes she forgets to add salt. It seems unlikely that she could exist this long without understanding something as basic as an electric stove top, but people always cooked for her, or there was always Whole Foods for prepared meals and buffets. She could always get by.

At least she learned to drive.

29

Following an arduous drive from Holbeach to Copley Square, Teresa stops at a PUG by South Station and washes her hands twice to cleanse herself momentarily of the filth in the nest. She checks in for a lunch break on the app. A lunch break at nine in the evening—whatever, that's her workday and her head and stomach both need it. It is a muggy evening in June and there is commotion inside: people getting off their trains and hiding out in the station for a shot of air-conditioning. She takes a moment to browse some of the new books at Jimmy's Newsstand. *Holistic Apex* is no longer in stock. The bookstore is unusually crowded, as people have moved inside from an even larger crowd on the way to the platforms by Sundry Meadows and the Au Bon Pain. All service on buses and trains has been postponed for an hour.

Teresa walks through frenzied crowds and hears

murmurs about a "bomb scare" and a "possible active shooter." Men in suits cry on their phones that Amtrak can't take them home to New York. People are shouting over other people shouting. Ordering taxis. Ordering planes and hotel rooms. It begins to rain. While everyone is dry inside the station, the weather adds a sense of urgency to the situation.

Someone orders a CR.

"Now how come they got the windshield wipers going if it's a self-driving car?" she hears someone say when the passenger gets in. "Or driverless. Or the fuck they call this."

Teresa stares at the CR, wondering who is inside. Someone calls to her. "Hey. I know you." It is a voice of fond accusation.

Teresa turns around. One of the Bethanys from All-Over stands by the departure board with a turquoise carry-on that matches her turquoise gym dress and sandals. Bethany's face telegraphs disappointed identification. She must have mistaken Teresa for a friend from university or a former neighbor.

"You were at Render Falls, right?" It isn't clear whether Bethany remembers what part of the building Teresa worked in. Nevertheless she says she is about to grab dinner in a way that suggests Teresa should join her. They walk together toward the soup and salad place by the exit.

Her name isn't Bethany but Nico; she was promoted

six months ago to work with the user research team down in Washington.

The AllOver staffer orders a glass of white wine and continues to talk. It is difficult to maintain apartments in San Francisco and DC, but this is what makes sense for her right now, given how much time she spends on the West Coast. Her plants are high-maintenance and she hasn't had much luck with plant-sitters. She met Fal Guidry for the first time recently in person. "Inspiring guy. Nice-looking too. I can tell why Vermont likes him." She whispers that the company is in talks to acquire the rideshare app PickUp.

"Fal's a bold man." Nico leans into the table and whispers again, "And Vermont, well. They're . . . you know. Hush-hush at the moment." She raises an eyebrow and appears proud to break the gossip. "Verm's old too, like eleven years older than he is. Plum is her daughter, but I bet you could guess just by looking at them." She laughs and holds her glass by the stem. "It's a family business."

"What about her father?" Teresa asks.

The Bethany looks confused. "Plum Sasha's? Some VC guy."

"Vermont's father. George Honey Q."

Nico frowns. "I don't know who that is."

The high-top chairs aggravate the pain in Teresa's lower back. She continues to nod her head as Nico talks about some of her coworkers. "The hottest guys are all in the Chicago office, maybe tied with Seattle, but definitely not the Pacific Northwest writ large. In DC, the men are more clean-cut and preppy, which I don't mind but it's a little old-fashioned. The guys there usually want to go on *real* date kind of date situations and I like to keep things more relaxed. I expect a man to wait for me. I can't do the whole wait-three-days-before-responding-to-a-text kind of pomp and circumstance. That's for girls who don't take their careers seriously and are in for the ring. *Any* ring. You know what I mean?"

When the check arrives, Teresa waits a beat, wondering if Nico will expense it. Instead Nico looks at her. "Split down the middle?" Teresa didn't have any wine and Nico had three glasses. It is easier to say nothing. The waitress returns with the bill folder containing paper receipts for their AllOver transactions and one pen.

Nico rolls her eyes as she grabs for the pen. "Waste of paper. You'd think a restaurant in Boston would have it together."

Teresa glances at the receipt across the table. Nico left nine dollars for a tip. She hands Teresa the pen, and Teresa jots down the same. She looks at Nico's receipt at the center of the table again. Nico left five dollars for a tip, but Teresa mistook it for a nine upside down. Teresa slides her receipt underneath Nico's and closes the bill folder.

They walk out of the restaurant and a CR is waiting

for the Bethany. She reserved a hotel for the night even though the South Station trains are running again. Nico waves when she steps into the blue pod and Teresa wonders who might be driving it. Someone she knows. Maybe someone from high school. Or it could be Nichelle or Abril or someone else from training that she liked. Teresa feels like she has betrayed those temporary friends of hers from training. Why didn't she try to keep in touch? It's always hard to make friends at work.

She turns the corner and sees another blue pod, which is much smaller. A CR but a quarter-size. Child-size. The mini-CR circles South Station in the bike lane at about five miles an hour. Teresa jogs over to it as the object approaches. It looks like a little blue bug, the size of a Big Wheel. Who could even fit inside . . . a baby could. A baby seer—the hell? She stands with her arms and legs outstretched to the width of the bike lane. The little CR chugs forward and backs up when it approaches her.

"Can you hear me?" Teresa shouts. The CR tries to move forward without straying outside the lines of the bike lane. It attempts to outmaneuver Teresa, but she stands in its path once again.

Again, the baby CR backs up. It reverses and dodges from her, stopping before the sidewalk. Teresa charges for the CR. She reaches for the hood, hoping she has the strength in her grip to open the nest. But it's smooth on top, no seams at all. There is no way to enter it. The baby

CR zooms forward at twice its ordinary speed and out-
runs her.

She picks up another five passengers after her break.
She is quiet on a truck ride home, and when she moves,
in the privacy of her own apartment, she feels like she is
radiating pain. Not physical pain, but psychic, the hol-
low lows; the low of the nest, and what it says of her—it
seems to follow her everywhere. She feels toxic, ashamed,
stammering, even at a coffee shop counter, unsure why
anyone would ever speak to her at all or take her order.
Day becomes night again. She can't remember the last
time she saw her mother. She realizes, if she should ever
lose her apartment, she could sleep in a PUG; not com-
fortably, but it is safe and private. Shelter is shelter and
there's a roof over her head when she's in it. No shower,
but she could use the facilities at the Y, if it ever came to
that.

What would happen if she fell further? If AllOver
fired her, where would she go? With her mother forever, a
job in Brixboro? No one wants her. Finally she understands why it is harder to get a job as you get older: it is not
lack of motivation, but experience of the sort that a résumé never reveals. She will never walk into a job interview with the look of someone hopeful and innocent,
who believes the doors to the future are open to everyone
and just.

At her night, in the afternoon day, she crawls into bed

and hugs her knees as she searches online for information about the baby CR. The "CRgoCart" is what AllOver calls it. She finds the press release. Right now it offers taco deliveries within a two-mile radius from South Station. It's fully automated, they say. But so is the CR, they say. Kids will grow up expecting this to be the nature of cars: some kids grow up to be passengers, others play seer.

t's sunrise. Teresa parks in a PUG by the water near Castle Island. In the distance are kiteboarders flying out from the bay to the sky in spirals on their boards. Cleaning the passenger seats, she finds a Dunkin' Donuts bag with a half-eaten bagel wrapped in wax paper. She tucks the bag under her arm as she steps outside. The sky is brilliant with shades of lavender that she only sees in dreams. It plunges in ribbons sinking into the water. The traffic behind her sounds like wind.

She pats the sparkling sides of the PUG. The texture makes her think of the grooves on a climbing wall. With the Dunkin' bag under her chin, she grips the PUG, fingers splayed. Her feet light as she moves upward, slow and spiderlike, she makes her way to the top.

It's not much of a bagel. Thin and much too soft and coated with a puttylike daub of cream cheese. She eats the last of it anyway. Orange and mauve colors wail over the ocean, bright and open, endless. The gleaming brass-hardware sun looks like a lock to a door to the edge of the world. The sounds of the motors of the very early commuters from a highway off in the distance remind her that she is not alone. She hungered for silence for so many years. It's quiet in the CR. Sometimes. But it's boring when it's quiet. What a dreamy view. AllOver could have built their garages as facsimile sedimentary rocks that camouflage into any environment. Instead, the PUGs dazzle like this sunset. This is their Plymouth Rock. Bold and majestic, unlike the real Plymouth Rock. It's All-Over's, but the sunset and this moment are hers alone.

Teresa looks at the shimmering blocks between her knees. The surface inhales the colors of the sky and bounces back its own version of orange, purple, and pink. At other times of day, the PUG roof might have been too hot to sit on, too hot for her fingertips to grip. If she sits too long, the texture will impress the pattern into her skin. Inside the CR and inside the PUG, she's the ugly thing, the worm of a hermit crab—an eyesore without a pretty house to hide under. Outside it, she's queen of a precious rock. The colors of the sky are arms reaching out to carry her home.

Her birthday is coming up. She'll do nothing again. No one remembered last year except for old yoga studios and hair salons in Brooklyn and Cambridge that emailed her 10 percent off coupons for her next visit. Even her mother forgot. Teresa came home with pizza. She and her mother had the pizza on paper plates that read "Congrats 2020 Grad" in rainbow color letters and confetti print that she got at Job Lots in 2026. After the TV show ended, her mother said, "Oh, it's today, isn't it?"

In a few years, she will be twenty thousand days old, but not this year. On her ten thousandth day of existence, Sinisa surprised her with a cupcake at work. "Ten thousand days is important," he said. "Ten thousand nights of sleep." Twenty thousand nights of sleep is a good milestone to have in sight.

She reaches for her phone, passcode 7485, and turns on the radio. There's a familiar chime. It's the public radio morning show. It begins with a segment about working women, and Vermont Qualline is the guest.

"We meet again, Vermont," Teresa says to her phone and no one else.

The woman's voice is sharp and violet. "Know your worth," she says to the host. "Women are raised to settle and sell themselves short. I instruct all the women who work with me to negotiate, negotiate." Vermont talks about the team of women that she mentors, and all the women she has hired and watched blossom through their careers at AllOver. *Forbes* magazine said AllOver has the best parental leave policy in all of Silicon Valley. This is all thanks to her hard work and persistence and unwavering commitment to the Holistic Apex. "It's about taking control over your life. Women are too afraid of control, too demure, but you have to grab life by the horns if you're in it to win it—and I am."

The host asks Vermont about the company's recent scandal. Falconer Guidry offered free CR rides to anyone in Los Angeles who needed to evacuate in the wildfires. He rescinded the offer before it could begin, due to "unexpected infrastructural demands and limited capacity" and donated five million dollars to the Red Cross to make amends.

"Okay, but that's Fal, and I am myself. Why are you asking me this?"

"He's the head of your company."

"Yes, and Fal is his own person. I had no hand in what he did. Talk about the problems working women have to deal with. Taking the blame for mistakes that men make is high on the list!"

The host drops it. "Could you tell us more about the self-driving car fleet? It's quite a technical achievement."

"Actually, the CR is driverless, not self-driving technology. There's a difference," Vermont says. "And yes, this is the first rollout of automotive technology that can navigate autonomously through all environments and any precipitation. No other autonomous vehicle can move end to end through cities, let alone a city in the rain. Or a city beset with wildfires. We have the only driverless vehicle fleet prepared to face the reality of the climate crisis."

Teresa shuts off the radio app and removes her shirt. She'd like to throw her phone into the water. Watch it skim and slip like a pebble in ducks and drakes. She'd tumble in the dunes and grass honeyed in the sun, roll around in the sun's warmth and make a home there in the field between the highway and the ocean with all the filthy seagulls. A home without a phone. Just sky, sunrise, and open water; and this magic rock, an invitation to everything in the world that is of any importance. Another splash of light breaks into broad morning sky. It is time to go home.

But first, she dives into the water.

er free time she spends shopping online. For kitchen items and useless things. She ordered a small piece of peacock ore because she remembered wanting it from the Museum of Science gift shop as a child, even though her father had said it was a waste of money.

Yesterday, the bike she ordered arrived, and today there's a package containing a ring. It's a sideways egg like the one she loved at Cedars, but the stone is an opal not a garnet. "All . . . Over Oval Opal," she says aloud as she slides the ring on her left middle finger for the first time, alone in her dark apartment.

And she orders penny loafers like the pair she wore in high school. She used to slip T tokens in the folds. On the weekends when the commuter rail was slow to run, she would take the bus to the Quincy Adams subway station and hand a five-dollar bill to the old man with the Santa

Claus beard who was always sitting at the counter behind scratched glass. He was so careful with the tokens, which he organized in tall stacks. He would count out five tokens and roll them over to her through a narrow chute. One token to ride the Red Line to Harvard Square, one for the ride back, three for her change purse to save for another day, which didn't happen—two of those tokens went in her penny loafers.

In the fridge is a small dish of lasagna. She made and shared a larger dish with Patti earlier in the evening. This dish is for her mother. She'll rent a car on Sunday morning, as she does every week, return to Brixboro, and help out around the house for the day.

She's scrolling Petfinder on one tab, pausing to read about a family of beagles—their rib cages visible under their thick coats, their eyes gentle and blank—sheltered at the Blue Hills Rescue League. Some of the dogs in the picture are grown puppies, but their mother she wonders about. "This old gal doesn't ask for much. She gets anxious in new places but she's fiercely loyal if you show her love," the listing reads. Just like me, Teresa thinks.

There's a free pass to the Museum of Fine Arts on her desk that she picked up from the library. She'll take the commuter rail into town to visit next Friday. She looks up Sinisa—she can't help it. It is the same as ever: pages and pages for some accountant in Ljubljana and a basketball coach in Belgrade. Sinisa never bothered with social media. Never set up a personal site. All there is in all the

World Wide Web is one page of staff bios for the laboratory. A thumbnail jpg and a list of his degrees. He looks good. He looks like she always imagined he'd look like when they got to be this age.

He'd been so easy to be around. The way, when she first moved into the Inman Square place, after he'd wrap up studying real late, he'd join her on the couch—what she still thought of at the time as his couch—and say, "What's going on in that quick mind of yours?" Like she was the one with the life.

And he cooked most nights. Risotto and salads on the weekends for lunch, when Fluffernutter on white bread would have been enough. It was something she didn't think much to appreciate; at the time, it seemed like just another task for the day that got done.

Nothing in the car he drove to California would have survived this long. Cardboard boxes would have been the first to go, but suitcases have finite life spans too. What else did he have: Faith No More CDs in jewel cases, cotton shirts that wouldn't hold up after three hundred washes. That copy of *Lanark*, maybe he did get around to reading it, or it was donated somewhere, or it sits on his bookcase, forgotten, but still a belonging. And the dog was an old dog the last time she saw them both.

There was a lot she didn't know about Sinisa even when they lived together. He went to an Eastern Orthodox church somewhere around Fenway and kept that whole part of himself private. Sinisa could have another dog now. He didn't have much of a family or care much to meet hers more than a few holidays when the timing worked; but a family of his own seems like something that would have happened for him. In his life, since she knew him, there has been enough time for a whole new life to have been made, one more firmly grounded with determinateness and necessity than the years of potential and warm silences that they had together.

There had been things she could say to him about herself and what she wanted. Memories she shared with him that she hasn't told anyone since, not because these are big secrets but because there was no one else who would have cared. Things like how excited she was when she was eight or nine and rode the T into Boston with her father to watch the marathon, or why she didn't like biology class in college. She misses that; the practice of turning the water in her mind into words. Now these thoughts sort of simmer into steam before evaporating.

And still she's never been to California. Maybe she could do that. Fifty dollars a week goes directly into her savings account now. Maybe she could do something with it. She could act, for once in her life or at least for a long while, a little bit greedy. A little bit reckless. Take a vacation, maybe not to California—but to a place that could be special for her. She could visit the Azores and County Cork, Galway and Cape Verde. Find some long-lost relatives, sign up for one of those ancestry websites that puts you in touch with distant cousins.

Maybe it would be enough to check into a hotel nearby for a night, wrap herself in a hotel robe and watch movies on HBO that she wouldn't otherwise care to see. Teresa inspects a scratch on her wrist and thinks the veins look like interstate highway lines. Then she remembers the freeway called the "central artery" and realizes this is not an original thought.

Her prom date died in Afghanistan. She'll never know where he could have went. Lance from the Brooklyn Modern lives in DC now and works at the Smithsonian. There was a Matt and a John in college, and a few others; they show up as names and ages and addresses in website databases that trigger pop-up ads. Next to one name, she will see an age that sounds right and an address somewhere like Amesfield or Marshfield or Kingston, which she'll know is the one. Sometimes a LinkedIn page that says math teacher at Brockton High or captain at Weymouth Fire Department. If any of them googled her back, they'd find watermarked party photos on proprietary websites from gallery openings she attended for several strange years; Teresa, looking uncomfortable but not out of place, necessarily, beside people she will never see again. Never face-to-face.

On another tab is her retirement account. It's been ten years since she's thought about it, and there's more in the account than what she imagined, but not nearly as much as the websites say she should have saved by this age. Here is something tangible that she has taken from MassTech and the Brooklyn Modern. It's luck, and only luck, that she was able to have and forget something like this. She enters her account and routing numbers. Now fifty dollars will automatically transfer each week. She'll increase it once she's ready. She'd like to retire, eventually.

Teresa clicks on graphs and estimates and a list of company names that are among the fund's largest investments. Her retirement account tracks the S&P 500. Something else that she doesn't understand. Under Apple and Microsoft, Berkshire Hathaway and Johnson & Johnson, there's AllOver—OVAA. It's 5 percent of the index fund holdings. Near the bottom of the website are links to the holdings in the news. "Meme stock or value play? Experts tell us AllOver is both."

Teresa is now a member of the Old Colony YMCA in downtown Stoughton. Where she first learned to swim. She was only a baby, but if she tries hard she thinks she can remember those floating laps with her mother in the pool in the basement. Reach and pull. Reach and pull. She bought new goggles for the occasion with the hopes that these wouldn't leak. The pool is colder than the water in Brookline or Brixboro. It feels smaller than the last time she set foot in this location.

In no time she has covered a mile's worth of laps. Lap thirty-nine. A good job at thirty-nine. She worked in the communications department at an insurance company in the Pru. Two months' cover for someone on maternity leave.

She had a great boss. They were the same age, but he got married when he was nineteen and had kids and seemed older. Well, maybe not older. But talking to him was like talking to someone from the past. He seemed to have been teleported in from the 1960s. The logistics of his life were bewildering. For one thing, he was supporting a family with six kids on a salary that was more than what she made, of course, but in a job like he had, there was no way he was clearing six figures. He met his wife at a Congregational church in Somersworth, New Hampshire, where they still live and still go, only now as a party of eight. A house with eight humans. She didn't even have eight friends she could invite over for a dinner party. Her brain couldn't process what Scott's commute had to have been like or the age of his oldest child, who was born when they were both twenty-one. When he mentioned his oldest son, she tried calculate to thirty-nine minus twenty-one but her mind delivered null. She wondered what kind of car he drove or did they take two vehicles everywhere. Did they walk to church at least?

His house, she imagined, had to be a place full of life, with all the freckly children in the photos on his desk running through doorways at all hours. And signs of them everywhere even in their absence: a worn-out catcher's mitt above the microwave, a hot pink Hula-Hoop looped over the mailbox, that sort of thing.

Her second week at work, she had unusual and

unbearable cramps, which presented a problem—not just in the pain in her side, but how to explain why she needed to skip out of work without wanting to tell Scott what kind of doctor she needed to see or for what complications.

"I'm sorry, I have another appointment at eleven," she told him. "I thought I'd take an early lunch, but it is possible, if things are busy at the doctor's, it could take two hours. Also, I am really sorry, I don't know how many more appointments I might need after this. I might have to go in for a full day at some point, but I can definitely work around that. If you need me to, I can take work home on Saturday and make up for it."

"Sure. No problem," he said.

"I could get a note," Teresa said, "if I need to get that full day off."

"A note?" Scott looked fully puzzled. "From me? Okay. What kind of note do you want me to write?"

She realized then that all she had to do was let him know where she would be and that was all he asked for, because he never doubted that what she said was true. Still, she phrased her email to him about her appointment to remove the uterine cysts and a day to recover after surgery in the vaguest way possible and as a request for permission. "If it's okay, I'm going to book another doctor appointment next week that will take all day. Also, the doctor thinks I should possibly take the day after that off to recover if that's not a problem. It might be another day after that. I'm not sure yet. But I'll try my best to schedule the appointment on a Friday."

"No problem. Just let me know what days off you need," he emailed back in five minutes.

What a great job that was. She was trusted.

ot yet dark and early in her shift. It's busy,
even for Friday rush hour, and she can't understand why. There is a single lamp blazing
bright in the window of a fifth-floor apartment out by Alewife. Teresa's attention lingers on it as
she waits for the light to turn green. That's someone's
home. What would it be like to have a nice one-bedroom
apartment there?

The light turns green. Cars behind the CR begin to
honk. Don't they know they're honking at a driver who
isn't there? She never noticed she has no horn herself until now.

"Think I should write a screenplay?" says a woman to
her husband, going from from Salem to Charlestown. It
is an older couple. Retirees, probably. They spend the entire ride scheming up "storyboards and scenes."

"Don't forget characters and character arcs," the

husband says. "A good screenplay needs a compelling protagonist."

"How about someone like me?" she replies.

He winks at her.

The next passenger travels from Cambridge to Quincy. It's a quicksand on I-93 South. There is no good time to drive south on 93. Driving north isn't a picnic but it is scenic. To your right is the bay and there are boats out at all hours. Even in bad weather. The highway is on a hill. You chug up and away and then finally there you see it, off in the distance, a 140-foot-tall gas storage tank with rainbow stripes like a giant toddler took a paintbrush to it. Sister Mary Corita Kent did that. She was a nun who learned to silk-screen inspired by Warhol; a pacifist and anti–Vietnam War activist. The Rainbow Swash is the sign that you are leaving Quincy and Boston is coming up. It might be coming up in five minutes if you happen to be driving at, say, three a.m. on a Saturday night; or you might wait another twenty minutes for the Boston cityscape to appear before you, just up that way, right up the hill. This beautiful city is ahead of you and soon.

Even in the worst traffic, worst possible weather, the city opens up to cars driving in from the south. It appears, bright and shiny on either side of the highway, extending like open arms. In the seventies and the eighties, commuters would have to leave home by seven or eight. By the nineties, the same workers had to set out by five or six. Now the morning traffic begins at four a.m. Generations have tried to outwit a highway that has never been and will never be easy—especially on the ride back. Driving south feels like the arms of the city push you out; you are shoved from the jangly city chaos to the car soup of the suburbs. Instead of water, there is a sea of big-box stores to the right. It is noisier on this side of the highway and there's endless construction.

You might find yourself thinking, hey, I can get from Central Square to Quincy in ten minutes. Especially if you have just moved to Braintree or Weymouth or even Scituate and found yourself working hard to keep in touch with friends in the city that you have left behind. You get home to your place in ten minutes, maybe fifteen, and you tell your friends, the South Shore is not so bad. One time this will happen. And you will tell everyone you live ten minutes outside of Boston. When the truth is you live an average of seventy minutes outside of Boston. An hour, two hours' drive from Boston. Fifteen miles away, close in theory, but that ten-minute drive that happened that one time will never happen again. Soon enough you'll be fighting the traffic and cursing the city madness. There are no backroads to beat this. Wait forty-five minutes without lifting your foot from the brake pedal. You live there now.

On the way out, by 93 South, is the old John Hill Mint. In the eighteenth century, Hill had his sixteen-year-old daughter step on a balance scale. He added silver shillings piece by piece to the other basket until the weights were level. That became the girl's dowry. The Old

Mint is brick, like every other building around here, but with a gold gambrel roof and ornate cupola that shows it has some history. It's a Whole Foods today.

Teresa is stuck in that traffic now with nothing to look at but the man watching MSNBC on the flat-screen and resting his feet on the opposite seat. He's eating a sandwich and drinking coffee. She can see Sister Corita's tank in her rearview as she curls off the highway exit. Ahead of her is a luxury car that shares her name. Teresa blinks. No, it's a Tesla.

People are out on the streets. Groups and individuals. More than she's ever seen in neighborhoods like this. They move like they are headed to a parade or a county fair but no one has lawn chairs. She drives past a group of guys in basketball jerseys. They stand by the sidewalk, one with a basketball under his arm. The park where they shoot hoops appears to be closed. Farther along the sidewalk are a few people with their dogs who have evacuated the dog park.

The traffic on the street is relentless. At an intersection where six roads intersect, managed by a triple-sided light instead of a rotary, which is uncommon in this part of town, there's a cop in the center waving cars through, while the other five cars hold up and wait their turns. When it's Teresa's time to go, she notices how backed up all the other roads are; this isn't rush-hour-in-the-suburbs traffic. It's get-the-fuck-out-now-every-car-for-miles traffic.

There's smoke in the sky and a billboard to the right over a mess of cars. "Take the T," the sign says, with the T in the subway circle logo. The passenger has switched to Channel 7 nightly news. Teresa turns the sound on in the passenger unit so she can listen too.

A news reporter live on the street is speaking with a city official. He tells her, "If you recall the gas explosions in Andover and Lawrence in 2019, this appears to be a similar unfortunate circumstance. This stuff happens in these old towns in New England. The infrastructure is old. People renovate the exteriors of the buildings, but the insides haven't updated much." The news reporter interjects, "Something interesting to know about Braintree and Randolph is this region was meant to be included in the city limits of Boston in 1912. There was a plan to incorporate everything within ten miles from Beacon Hill, but the old powerful families in the city didn't like the immigrants in the South Shore towns. Boston could have been one of the largest cities in the world."

Out on the street, she watches another crowd of people exit a dentist office in a nervous hurry. The dentists and dental hygienists check their phones and look upset. They wait in the parking lot. Another group of workers has come to join them. They have exited the same office building that looks like a house. Women in pantyhose, baggy skirts, and Keds look left and right, all confused. Everyone who was inside now stands out in cliques and clusters. All the cashiers at CVS and Burger

King. All the staff at an accountant's office and a nearby salon. Women in Lycra run out of the spin class studio, sweaty and pink, with towels wrapped around their necks. Tenants crowd outside an apartment complex at the corner. One of the women is in pajamas with a bath towel wrapped around her head.

"Shit," the man inside the CR says to no one at all. He taps at his phone and sips the last of his Sundry Meadows coffee. Teresa hears a bling. The passenger has requested to stop here. It is faster for him to walk home. Or walk somewhere. She watches as he tries to make his way past clusters of people.

A window breaks. Shards of glass fall from a building onto the concrete. Office workers run in all directions, bumping into congregations of other workers.

The traffic is in an unbearable standstill. Drivers fail to form a path for the ambulance and fire trucks. The sirens remind everyone that however bad things are for them right now, it could be a lot worse.

There's an explosion. It looks like Sister Corita has painted over the sky.

Teresa inches the CR forward where she can. Beside her there's a karate class on the sidewalk with a bunch of kids in white uniforms. The workers from a doggie daycare hold a dozen leashes each while all the dogs are going nuts.

Another explosion. A cinder block flies from the roof of a three-decker and lands on the hood of an old Mercury

Mystique. The car spins left, crashing into the Ioniq in the lane next to it. Teresa can see the windshield is busted. The driver's head is motionless against his steering wheel.

A car behind Teresa tries to pass her. The driver recognizes this is a driverless vehicle. There isn't even a passenger inside anymore. This man in a Toyota Camry finds a narrow place between the CR and the Mystique. A car alarm bleats from behind. Teresa follows the Toyota. He's cleared a path. She follows him out of the ruckus and onto a desolate street. They emerge at another congested parkway. The tires of a Lexus screech as it cuts over the median strip to set off, still stuck, but facing the other direction.

A Prius crashes into a Jeep. The Prius bucks back into a guardrail and spins forward like a pinball, colliding with a Chevy Equinox. Another vehicle hits the CR. What would it be like to be seen, to give the least f— *asterisk*—cks? she wonders, pressing down on the gas pedal although her gut says she should brake. Ahead is a dead-end drive that looks like a runway, and in her frazzled imagination, Teresa wonders what it must have been like to be a kid watching the planes take off in the old airport that became an AllOver headquarters.

Teresa jams the distress signal when the CR starts spinning.

33

She would like to shake her life up like a snow globe. Let it all fly and settle wherever it will. This experience of soaring blind and weight-less with the earth beneath her is as close as she will get. It must be how the astronauts feel: to have your weight against a floor give way to a sense of an emptiness, alien atmosphere underneath your feet.

From the nest, Teresa, bloody where the chain mail snagged at her temples, feels the unit transform to a sledge. It slides from the top of the CR toward the median grass between highway ramps, where an AllOver drone catches it. She rips the Mylar space blanket from the sides of her capsule and wraps herself in it. Incidents like this have to be what it's for. Her skin is smooth and itchy, incongruous like the weather outside. This discomfort feels substantial and adorned like a residue of endurance, but it is the ordinary trace of spring turning to summer on her body.

Where is she? Canton or Braintree. Braintree. Always a vivid mental picture when she'd see the town name on an MBTA map. Walnut trees were once all over the region. That's what her father used to tell her. Someone in the past called walnut trees "brain trees" and that's how the town and the subway stop got the weird name.

She's wrong. It's Stoughton. Not far from Render Falls. There never were any walnut trees around here either.

Just down the way a familiar halo of light illuminates the red and gold sky. It is the tangy acid air above land that was once Stuart Falls Memorial Airport. It was almost Ultra SystemsTech Electronics. Before that it was almost Teddy Sullivan Elementary School, and before that it was the Arnone Welting Factory, site of an industrial explosion and building collapse in 1907 that killed seventy-four workers, and before that nothing, a long time of nothing. Nothing, for many years, beyond and by the Praying Town atrocities, when people from here were forced out of their cultures and homes and were interned on Deer Island. Before King Philip's War, the land was homeland. Trees and swamp.

She's flying now in the nest, and in the rush she feels like she did as a little kid, jumping in piles of leaves or snow: how a child feels entirely inside their body while instinctively crashing into something new, something unknown. A thud and the motion stops. The way a kid can stand with their back to something and fall right into it.

Her back is in the leaves. Her back is in the snow. When she was little, when it snowed on Saturday or Sunday morning, her father would run outside with bowls to catch it. He'd heat up maple syrup and pour it over the fresh snow. The syrup was supposed to turn into taffy but her father never heated it long enough. She'd get up out of the snow pile for a bowl of sugar and snow. Spoonfuls of snow would melt to water on her tongue and she saved the maple syrup for last.

The drone deposits the nest on another median strip. Somersaulting out, her hair picking up trash and dead weeds, she lands against a WRONG WAY sign. There she hangs, still parked and immobile, one hand on a guardrail, the other digging at the thin grass. She feels lucky that her childhood was good. Nothing too scary or sad happened when she was young. Every memory from that time is something to hold, most of all, running with her brother in the snow or in those leaves. Falling into the piles, raked or shoveled. Falling back without fear. And she was good back then too. That's what one of the birthday letters from her father had said. "You were always such a quiet baby."

Another car passes by. A pearlescent van.

The van has red lights flashing. The lights look like sinewy devil horns and the reflective surface of the vehicle shimmers red as it journeys toward her. Out come EMTs or whatever they are, care workers of a sort, in milky pink scrubs with a milky pink gurney.

The house where she lived in Stoughton was across the way from an assisted-living facility. Trees and bushes obscured the building; all she could see out the window was a quiet lane. She never explored it. It looked like the people there wanted privacy, so she respected that. What she knew of it was the wood sign with its logo inside an illustration of the sun. Sometimes—quite often, too often—she'd notice a red light flashing in the trees and an ambulance would emerge. She'd pray in silence for whomever it was in the ambulance that zipped away into the night.

The walls inside are a familiar jagged luster. White, shattered, and endless, dicing and replicating what surrounds in pearl logic. They have taken her to Render Falls.

She wishes she had asked Al Jin if he thinks he'll see the Wampanoag people before the land was taken and thus became Plymouth. Like it used to be. Or Paul Revere, hanging around Al's neighborhood, sometime well before the midnight ride, having an ordinary night out with his friends. And how about the witches in Salem; can he only go someplace in time that a photograph could have captured, or can he remember them too? Sacco on the shoe factory line—might he see that? Lizzie Borden down in Fall River; if he goes there, in off-hours, will he find evidence, at last, of whether Lizzie did it or not?

"Just keep breathing." Another Bethany. This one dressed like a nurse. She's wheeling Teresa through this

space of crystalline walls and silver flowers that are alive.
"What happened?"

"I made it to the Holistic Apex." She feels light-headed
and the sense that she is wearing goggles, about to dive
into something wet. "What I'd like is sugar and snow."
Teresa would like some sugar and snow. Render Falls,
above her, in swimming fits of color like the inside of an
abalone shell. It's quiet. Nourishing silence. She might be
looking at the world through goggles, but her hair feels
normal and there's no pinching at the nose bridge either.
There's a doctor. All is silent; whatever the doctor is saying is muffled to nothing in her ears, but her body knows,
her body is listening, and it hears that everything will be
okay. Tomorrow is her birthday. Seventeen thousand plus
nights of sleep. She will call her mother. She could text
Al. Or maybe she won't. She has an apartment to go back
to and a job that is safe.

Teresa can't wait to drive again. What a great job.
She'll be okay once she gets back home.

Acknowledgments

Greatest thanks to my editors, Ben Brooks and Sean McDonald, and to my agent, Sarah Bowlin. Thanks to Brendan Byrne for the early read and for helping me name the "CR." Thank you to everyone at MCD and FSG who worked on this book, including Abby Kagan, Andrea Monagle, Bri Panzica, Chris Allen, Claire Tobin, Debra Helfand, Nina Frieman, Susan Bishansky, and tracy danes. Thank you, friends. Thank you, family.